A Very Cerberus Christmas

A Cerberus Novella
Marie James

Copyright

Cerberus MC

New to the Cerberus MC?
Each book is a standalone with a continuing subplot and can be read individually, but to get the most out of the series it's best to read in order.
Book 1:https://books2read.com/Kincaid
Book 2. https://books2read.com/Kid
Book 3. https://books2read.com/Shadow-Cerberus-MC-Book-3
Book 4. https://books2read.com/Dominic-Cerberus-MC-Book-4
Book 5. https://books2read.com/Snatch
Book 6. https://books2read.com/Lawson-Cerberus-MC-Book-6
Book 7. https://books2read.com/Hound
Book 8. https://books2read.com/Griffin-Cerberus-MC-Book-8
Book 9. https://books2read.com/Samson-Cerberus-MC-Book-9
Book 10. https://books2read.com/Tug-Cerberus-MC-Book-10
Book 11. https://books2read.com/Scooter
Book 12. https://books2read.com/Cannon
Book 13. https://books2read.com/Rocker
Book 14. https://books2read.com/Colton-Cerberus-MC-Book-14
Book 15: https://books2read.com/DrewCerberus
Book 16: https://books2read.com/JinxCerberusMC-
Book 17: https://books2read.com/ThumperCerberus
Book 18: https://books2read.com/ApolloCerberus

Want to binge the series? Grab this discount priced box sets!
Box Set 1: https://books2read.com/CerberusBoxSet1
Box Set 2: https://books2read.com/CerberusBoxSet2
Box Set 3: https://books2read.com/CerberusBoxSet3

Chapter 1

Lucy

I've ignored a lot over the years. It's a skill I mastered long before I got out of high school. Okay, maybe ignored isn't the right word. Maybe I've learned to not be affected by things is a better way to explain myself because I definitely see the stares each day when I pull up to the school in my ten-year-old car. I notice the cringes on the other parents' faces and the way they lean their heads in to gossip with moms on the PTA when they see me coming. My child is well behaved, gets good grades, and is very helpful. He's kind and courteous to other kids and always has a smile on his face. He's gracious and sweet. And he's still *that* kid. The child parents warn their kids to stay away from.

He's poor. His clothes aren't designer. Our car isn't shiny and new. He's carrying the same backpack in first grade that he carried last year in kindergarten. It's as if the parents are afraid if their children acknowledge him, his poverty is going to rub off on them and their investments will take a hit overnight. It doesn't matter how awesome my child is, he's never going to be accepted because of my income level.

If I could change it, I would, but short of winning the lottery, it's not going to happen. I can't even afford to play, and I'd never gamble away the little money we have on chance.

I give my little guy a huge genuine smile when my old clunker pulls up next in line. The teacher frowns when she sees me. She has to take extra caution to walk him around to the driver's side of my car to help him in because the rear passenger door doesn't open.

"Have a good day," she says with little sincerity before walking away, her head shaking as she looks at the other teachers helping with car pickup.

Harley smiles from the back seat, his cheeks pink from standing in the cold, waiting to be picked up.

"Hey, buddy. How was your day at school?"

"Amazing! Did you notice my new jacket?"

"I did," I say.

The jacket isn't exactly new, and I was waiting for him to mention it, wondering how he was going to react before speaking on it, but true to form, my child always finds the positive in everything.

"It has a pocket on the inside, but don't worry, I won't try to sneak a car to school in it."

He cuts his eyes out the window in a way that tells me I may have to check his pockets each morning.

The school-donated jacket is just another slap in the face, just another way for the school to tell me I'm a bad mother without actually coming out and saying those exact words. I've never sent my child to school hungry or cold. I'd go without before that ever happened, and I have, more than once, but sending him to school in layers to accomplish what he needs to stay warm must be just as bad a thing as nothing at all. I sent him this morning with a thermal t-shirt, a sweater and two hoodies. He was cozy. From the bulge of his backpack, I imagine he has traded most of those for the fleece-lined number he's now sporting.

I take a calming breath as I wait for traffic to die down enough for me to pull away from the school. It would be easy to point fingers and place the blame at someone else's feet, but I can own my own faults and choices in life. I was an active participant in my failures. Catching up is always harder than keeping pace, and although I don't regret a day I've had with Harley, I know parenting would be easier had I done it in the right order, namely, not falling in with a man who had no goals in life other than drugs, crime, and screwing over everyone he could before they caught on.

Robbie is different now, but there's not much the man can do behind the bars of prison. My relationship with Harley's father was off and on for years, and at any point, I could walk away, but I was as big of a mess and tangled up in the drugs as he was. If I were one to blame other people for my mistakes, I could point the finger at him for handing me that first joint, for prepping that first line of coke, but I was always looking for an escape. It was going to be him or someone else honestly, so there's no point in assigning blame. I thought it was love. Of course I did. I was young and looking for what I wasn't getting at home from my smothering parents. I was certain I found that in him.

I started to grow up; he never did. I said no to drugs after a couple of years because he was in and out of jail, and I didn't want that for myself, but I could never say no to him. I ended up pregnant; he landed in jail for five years with an additional eighteen months because he fancied himself a badass the first couple of months he was in and picked up more time.

I never kept Harley away from him. Once he started doing better, I started taking Harley to visit him. All our son has known is a dad behind bars, but that will end shortly because Robbie is scheduled to be released soon, and I have no idea how that's going to go. There's nothing between us any longer. Once both of us got fully sober, we both realized we have nothing in common, and neither of us is fool enough to think trying to work things out would be good for anyone, even for Harley's sake. But I won't keep our son from his dad.

"What did you learn today at school?"

"Nothing," he answers.

"We've talked about this," I say, my eyes on the road.

"Mom," he grumbles. "The other kids in class are working on high-frequency words, but I know them already."

"You didn't tell the teacher that, did you?"

I chance a glance at him in the rearview mirror.

"Of course not. I sat quietly and worked ahead in my math workbook."

This is something she could penalize him for later.

It's as if the teachers look for a way to cause problems for him out of spite. You'd think teachers would want to nurture his intelligence, but the ones at the school he's at seem to only want to keep him down, or at least at a lower level than kids with more money. Heaven forbid, the poor kid has a leg up somehow.

I pull into the gas station I know to have the cheapest gas.

"Can I trust you to stay in the car?" The cheapest gas also means the place isn't in the best neighborhood, and it's a gamble in whether it's safer to leave him in the car or walk him into the store. It also helps to stave off the guilt I'll feel from watching his eyes dart to the candy aisle, knowing he wants to ask for a piece. He never would. Somehow Harley knows we don't have the money. Maybe he's able to pick up on my stress from not having money even though I don't discuss such things with him. Maybe he hears other kids talking about our lack of it at school, but the child doesn't ask for things. He looks. I can see the want in his eyes. He's a kid after all, but he doesn't ask, and it kills me to not be able to give it to him. I do when I can, but it isn't often.

"Yes."

I lock the door, feeling confident in his answer because I lucked out with him. He's a very well-behaved child. It's like someone knew I needed calm and less challenging in my life.

The cashier sighs when she sees me coming, but I can't be the only person that comes in here and has to pay for gas with change. There are a lot of us in the neighborhood that have to do this very thing. Times are hard, and it's not just the economy right now. Life is freaking hard. The damn stock market could skyrocket and we wouldn't know. In the trenches, it's always going to be hard.

As I stand in line, I mentally calculate what we'll need between now and when I get paid on Friday, making sure we'll have enough so I can determine what I can put in the tank. I keep a few feet back from the person in front of me so I can keep my eye on my car. The line moves forward, and so do I. The cashier seems extra salty today, no smile on her face even though I've been coming here for years. The woman seems hell-bent on hating her job and everyone who steps foot in here. I decided long ago that she'll never build a rapport with anyone and gave up. She takes forever to count out my change as if I'm going to stiff her a dime on eight dollars in gas.

Having had my eyes off of him for longer than a minute, I'm in a hurry to get back out to the car, and my blood runs cold when I approach and don't see his form in the back seat.

"Harley!"

"It's an Indian, actually."

I jump at the masculine voice, and then startle further when I see the man the voice came from—dark beard down to his chest, bright blue eyes, bandana around the top of his head, full riding leathers, gloves on his hands.

Biker.

Bad news.

And he's standing beside my son.

Who is not in the car, but straddling a damn motorcycle. There are two others standing near, but neither speaks. Their presence feels like a warning. Bikers are known to travel in packs. I know this from experience. Where there's one, there's always a couple more lurking about.

"I told you to stay in the car," I snap.

I normally don't have to chastise my child. He's very well behaved, but right now I could twist his ear for not listening to me. I get that he's only six, and after this, I'll never leave him alone in the car again. I locked the door, worried about people getting in, not him climbing out, because he promised me he'd stay put. Leave it to the temptation of a motorcycle to draw him out. Where puppies may be the pull for others, damn bikes are his.

"Do you see this, Momma?" Harley leans forward, his arms too short to reach the handlebars, but he looks adorable as he tries. I don't think I've ever seen such a wide smile on his face.

I hate that I'm the one that's going to be the one to crush his good time, but the kid just doesn't understand the trouble he could be getting into. He doesn't know that his father got tangled up with bikers, and that's where all of Robbie's problems began.

"Harley, you—"

"Indian," the man says once again.

"His name is Harley," I hiss, not bothering to look over at the man.

"Really?"

I chance a glance at him. It's not really fair for a man with a wind-blown beard to have such an alarming smile. His leather vest is worn and well used—SNAKE—on a patch near his left shoulder. Charming. It seems like a warning, and one I'll heed.

"Get in the car," I tell Harley, reaching for him. I know how hot the parts of a motorcycle can get, and I don't want him burned. I just paid for gas with nickels and dimes. The last thing I can afford is a hospital bill.

"Listen to your momma, little man," the guy says when Harley looks up at me with pleading eyes, reluctant to end his fun so quickly.

I usher Harley into the backseat, nodding when he apologizes for getting out. I start to climb into the driver's seat, and nearly cuss out loud when I remember I stopped to get gas. For some people, driving off without getting their eight dollars in gas wouldn't be a big deal, but it would wreak havoc on our lives. I couldn't get to work or pick Harley up from school in the afternoons for the rest of the week.

"I can pump it for you," the man says, his smile still in place, despite how short I've been with him.

"I've got it," I tell him.

To his credit, the man doesn't reach for the gas nozzle, and he keeps his distance.

"He seems to really like motorcycles."

I start to pump my gas, keeping my back to him, but my eyes are on his reflection in the window. I don't know where his friends went, but I know they're around here somewhere.

"We're not bad guys, ma'am," he says. "We wouldn't hurt him."

I turn to face him at this declaration.

"So it's just normal for three bikers to talk to children when a parent isn't present?" I glare at him.

He smiles down at me, and I notice for the first time just how much bigger he is than me.

"I was swiping my card to get gas. I turned around, and he was sitting on my bike. Should I have picked him up and thrown him off? You showed up like fifteen seconds later. I can promise you, there wasn't anything creepy going on."

I swallow. It doesn't go unnoticed that he doesn't point out that I left my small child in the car alone. Many people would, and maybe it's natural to point the finger and blame others. I shove down the realization that these guys sound more like how Robbie is now—a changed man than the bikers he used to hang out with—and maybe that's just my own justification I'm trying to calm myself with for leaving my child and having him end up in a dangerous situation.

"Well, I'm sorry he bothered you."

"Didn't say he bothered me, ma'am."

The gas pump clicks off and despite the embarrassment it may cause, I hold the hose up just in case it helps. I don't know if it makes the gas left in the hose end up in my tank, but if it does, I'll take all that I can. I won't ever see this man again, and I refuse to let him derail my week.

"Thank you for not yelling at him. Have a good day."

I climb into my car and drive away.

Chapter 2

Snake

"You can't tell me you didn't see it coming," Skid says as he climbs off his bike, picking up the conversation right where it left off before we pulled away from the clubhouse.

Ace shakes his head. "Didn't have a clue."

"You haven't noticed the weirdness?" I ask.

"They were fighting. I figured it was because of Darby. Best guy friends fight over women all the time," Ace explains. "Hell, usually that's the only thing they'll fight over. That and if someone borrows money and never pays it back."

Skid nods in agreement.

"Who knew Itchy and Snatch were like falling in love and having a two-year lovers' quarrel?" Ace chuckles.

"Glad that shit is over," I mutter, but we all stand near our bikes for a long moment.

Itchy was shot on our last mission. We almost lost him, and that takes its toll on a team. It makes us realize, like a slap in the face, that despite how badass we are, we're also human.

"I think they're going to be happy together," Skid says, a twisted grin on his face.

"And y'alls budding relationship?" Skid asks, slapping me on the back.

I shake him off. "Shut the fuck up."

"What? Not going to be another happy Cerberus couple?"

"We were drunk," Ace grumbles. "Neither one of us were meant for sucking dick."

I shake my head. I always said I'd try anything once, and apparently I took that to heart. After a half a bottle of tequila that included trying a little man-on-man action with my best friend, we both learned very quickly that we weren't meant for the rainbow side of life.

Skid slaps me on the back with a chuckle.

"Hey, isn't that the chick's car from the gas station a few weeks back?" Ace asks as we walk toward the entrance of the diner.

Excitement fills my blood, and I walk a little quicker. Her fiery attitude hasn't been far from my thoughts, and after the shitstorm of Itchy getting hurt, I've been left wondering if I'd ever run into her again. People drive through town all the time. The station we stopped at to fuel up is on the highway, so there was a possibility that she was just passing through. Knowing she might be local makes my lips curl up into a smile as I tug open the door.

That smile immediately fades away as I enter and look around the dining room.

Harley, the cutest kid I've ever met, is standing up in a booth, his little chest puffed out as he faces two men. He doesn't look happy. His face is red, his little fists balled up like he's getting ready to punch them both in their noses.

The pretty woman has her hand on his shoulder, frustration drawing her brow in.

"She said she isn't interested. You need to leave," the little guy says, his voice a low growl, marked with his young age.

I know he's trying to sound intimidating, defending his mom, but he's all of forty pounds, tops.

Her eyes find mine, but the kid's back is to me as we approach.

The guys giving her a hard time spot us. The one in front has the wherewithal to widen his eyes just as Harley shifts his weight on the booth. I hitch my thumb to the right, telling the asshole to get lost. He sneers, but he must not be an idiot because he takes a hike. I watch as relief settles over Harley instantly. She pats his back, her eyes still on me, and I find that I like her looking at me. This time, she doesn't seem agitated with my presence like she did at the gas station.

But then there's a shift when I don't immediately walk away.

"See, Momma. I got this!"

The men didn't walk out of the diner. Maybe I'd leave her to her dinner if they did, but I wouldn't put it past two assholes like them to come right back once I stepped away.

"Hey there, little guy," I say to him once he settles down across from his mom. "Good looking out for your mom."

Harley turns in his seat to look up at me. His smile is wide when he spots me. Skid and Ace peel off, finding a table across the room. I may catch shit from them later, but they won't bother me while I'm trying to flirt with this woman.

"Hi, Snake," he says, reading the tag on my leather cut.

"Micah," I tell him, more for his mother's benefit as I hold out my hand for him to shake.

His hand is tiny in mine.

"Harley. This is Momma."

I chuckle as I release his hand and hold it out to his mother.

She looks down at it and I can see the battle in her eyes as she decides if she's going to stick with her anger from the gas station or give into courtesy.

"Lucy," she says after a long pause, but she never gives me her hand.

"Join us," the child says, and if it wouldn't be insanely inappropriate, I'd give the little guy a hug for the invite.

Lucy sighs, but she doesn't argue as I try to stuff my large frame into the booth. We always grab a table when we eat here, but I'm not going to argue that point right now.

"Why do they call you Snake?" Harley asks as he reaches for his glass of orange soda, his eyes wide with curiosity. I freaking love kids because I'll answer every single question he has with as many details as I can manage because I want Lucy to hear all of it. I could see in her eyes the moment we met that she had preconceived notions about bikers. Many people in town do. I want to prove her wrong about me and Cerberus as a whole.

"Well," I begin, "I was given that name in the Marine Corps. My last name is Cobreski, and the guys in my platoon weren't very original."

"That makes sense. I hate snakes, but I like you. How many motorcycles do you have?"

"Two, and one is a Harley."

"Really?"

The awe in his voice makes me smile. His joy makes his mother smile.

"Really."

"Will you let me ride on one?"

I look to her, knowing it would be a shitty thing to promise this kid something his mother would never allow to happen. Her head shakes only the slightest amount.

"That's not very safe, and I don't have a helmet small enough for you, little man. I'm sorry."

"Okay," he says with a tiny shrug.

Lucy clears her throat as if his quick agreement hurts her in some way. Most parents would feel relief at the lack of argument. I file it away, knowing there's more to this woman than what's on the surface. Although I normally wouldn't look twice at a woman that showed minimal interest in me, I find that I want to get to know more about her.

"So, you're in a motorcycle gang?"

I smile down at him.

"It's a club, not a gang." We often have to make the distinction, not that people really care what the differences are. "We do a lot of charity work and volunteering in the community. We help raise a lot of money. What school do you go to? We helped get some new playground equipment for Dolchester last summer."

"That's where I go! I love the new slide!"

The waitress swings by, dropping off a ton of food, and asking for my order. I look up at Lucy, once again making sure it's okay if I eat with them. She seems to have thawed a little because she doesn't scowl at me. I take it as a win and tell the waitress I want a burger and fries.

The conversation continues, Harley asking a million more questions around bites of grilled cheese and French fries. Lucy doesn't talk much other than reminders to Harley not to talk with his mouth full.

"I thought I heard you laugh from the kitchen!"

I stand when Edith approaches, my plate in her hand. She drops it on the table, her arms out a second before I wrap her in a hug. The elderly woman pats my back like she didn't just see me last week.

"How have you been, sweetheart?"

"Better now that I'm seeing you," she says as she steps out of my arms, her wrinkled hand cupping my bearded chin. "Where are your friends?"

I point across the restaurant to Skid and Ace, who each hold up a hand in a wave.

"Oh hi, dear. Are you two doing okay?" Edith asks, noticing Lucy and Harley.

"We're doing well," Lucy replies, a sweet smile on her face.

"I've got to get back to the kitchen before Luther burns it down. Tell that boss of yours and Emmalyn thank you for the Thanksgiving order." I take my seat as Edith scurries away, stopping by Ace and Skid's table for hugs before she heads into the kitchen to keep an eye on her husband.

"You know Edith and Luther?" Lucy asks, her first question of the afternoon.

"We've been coming here for years. Edith and Luther know everyone. Sweet people."

"They are," she confirms.

"They gave me a free slice of pie once when Momma didn't have enough money," Harley says.

"Harley," Lucy snaps, embarrassment pinking her cheeks.

"Really?" I say, looking over at the kid. "She didn't make you wash dishes? I left my wallet at home once too, and I had to scrub pots and pans all afternoon."

His eyes widen. "I didn't have to wash pots and pans. She must like me more!"

Lucy's eyes find mine, but they dart away quickly. I don't know if I helped the situation or hurt it more. I know she doesn't have a lot of money. Her car is proof of that, but she's gorgeous. She has a pretty awesome kid, and she's got an attitude that just draws me in for some reason.

The two guys that were harassing her give the waitress a hard time before getting up to leave, and I know Skid and Ace have eyes on them as they leave the diner. Hopefully, they're just a couple of assholes passing through.

The waitress stops by with the check, and I pull out my wallet.

"Together or separate."

"Together."

"Separate." Lucy glares at me.

"Together." I hand the waitress my card, and the girl just stands there confused until I nod at her to get moving.

"I can't let you do that."

"I interrupted your dinner. It's the least I can do."

"I'm capable of taking care of my child."

I lean against the back of the booth, my eyes on hers, and I pray she can see the sincerity in them. "I never said you couldn't. I appreciate the company and great conversation."

"With a six-year-old?" She scoffs.

"It was more mature than it would've been with those guys." I hitch my thumb toward Skid and Ace.

As if proving my point, those two idiots are having a competition on who can hold a spoon on their nose the longest.

"Looks like fun," Harley says as he notices what they're doing.

The waitress comes back with my card and take-home boxes for the food Lucy and Harley didn't eat. I sign the slip, leaving a generous tip. I should stand and leave, but when I look back at Ace, he shakes his head. The two guys that were giving her a hard time left the diner but they haven't left the parking lot.

I pull a couple of quarters from my pocket and hand them over to Harley.

"What are you doing?" Lucy snaps when I drop them into his hand.

"Hey, bud, why don't you go see what those machines have to offer," I tell him, pointing to the row of quarter machines on the far wall.

Harley looks to his mom, and she must see something in my eyes because she nods to him. He bounds over me, excited to have a fist full of quarters, and hauls ass toward the machines.

"I'm going to follow you home."

"The hell you are," she snaps, leaning over the table.

It's clear she wants to get her point across without others hearing her. I love that she doesn't feel any sort of obligation toward me, despite the fact that I just paid for her meal.

"Do you know the two men who were giving you a hard time when I walked in?"

Her eyes dart in the direction they were sitting. "I've never seen them before, but they're gone now."

"They're still outside," I tell her.

"How do you know?"

"I just do. My guys are going to stay here and make sure you aren't followed. I'm going to make sure you get home safely."

"And how do I know I'm safe with you knowing where I live?"

"I'm not a bad guy, Lucy, but I can promise those men can't say the same thing."

Her eyes search mine, and I bet she's going over every word that has come out of my mouth today, my interaction with her son, and the way Edith wrapped her arms around me.

"I won't even get off my bike, but I want to make sure the two of you get home safely."

"And if we have other plans?" she challenges.

"Do you?"

She shakes her head.

"I got tattoos! Do you have tattoos, Micah?"

"Quite a few, little man," I tell him, not pulling my eyes from Lucy.

Her gaze drops, eyes roaming over me, and I'm smiling when she discovers that I caught her looking.

"Okay, Harley. Let's go."

I block her before she can leave the diner, and somehow I manage without touching her. It's an easy thing to do since she seems so aware of me. Ace and Skid head out first, angling their bikes so the assholes would have to run over them to back their truck out. I wait patiently on my bike for her to pull out before following close behind her. I know the guys will give us several minutes to put some miles between us and the diner before they move. It may piss the guys who were bothering them off, but Ace and Skid know how to handle themselves.

Chapter 3

Lucy

I don't accept favors. I hate owing people, being indebted to them, especially men. Men want one thing because they're capable of doing everything else for themselves.

Micah "Snake" Cobreski, former Marine turned Cerberus biker, has now forced two favors down my throat. First was paying for dinner, and now because I was scared for my and Harley's safety, he's offered protection on our drive home. Other than coming out of the gas station a couple of weeks ago to Harley being on the stranger's bike, he hasn't done or said anything creepy, but still, trust doesn't come easily if it ever comes at all.

But as I drive home, trying to keep my eyes safely on the road ahead of me, I realize I'm not so much worried about him as a person and what his expectations are for those favors he's thrust upon me, I'm worried about what he thinks of me or what he's going to think of me once he sees where we live.

His bike is nice, and it's one of two he claims he owns. I bet he lives in a nice house. The one Harley and I rent is near shambles by any standards, but it's the best I can manage.

If I didn't get the feeling he's the type of guy to make sure I step inside safely before driving off, I'd pull up to a nicer neighborhood and flag him on. If those creeps hadn't had the nerve to say horrible things to me in front of my son, I would've put up more of a fight when he insisted on following me to safety while making sure those guys wouldn't find out where we live.

"Can we do these tattoos tonight, Momma?" Harley asks from the backseat.

"Sure," I tell him, my eyes going back to the rearview mirror.

We're at a red light, and just as he promised, Micah is right behind us. I pray my car doesn't stall out on us. Traffic is heavy, but it always is the day after Thanksgiving. Everyone is starting off their holiday shopping with a bang, spending money like crazy and going overboard. I didn't get paid until today, and it was our Thanksgiving celebration at the diner.

The interruptions from those two jerks ruined it, and I haven't decided yet if Micah's "rescue" was a positive or a negative.

I cringe as I pull into the driveway, trying to see what a newcomer would see as I look at our house. The yard is clean. The only thing on the front porch is Harley's neon green soccer ball. Even that we got used from Goodwill. Winter has killed the grass, and honestly, that's a blessing because I always have trouble keeping it cut. Gas money for the car is a big enough struggle without having to worry about sparing some for the neighbor's mower when he's feeling generous enough to let me borrow it.

I climb out, my eyes darting all over as Micah pulls his motorcycle up along the curb. As promised, he doesn't climb off his bike. He doesn't even power the thing off, and I take comfort in the low growl of the machine as Harley climbs out. At least I don't have to have any further conversation with the man. I make sure to lock my car because around here, anything will get stolen. Hell, even the locks sometimes aren't enough of a deterrent.

I give him a quick wave of gratitude, and Harley does the same before we climb the three steps onto the front porch. Before I can remind Harley about the screen door needing to be fixed, his excitement about getting inside and applying those tattoos make him forgetful, and he swings open the door and the wind catches it. The top hinge pops free, just like it did earlier today.

I know Micah watches it happen because the rumble of his motorcycle dies. With one hand on the screen so the thing doesn't completely fall away, I turn around to face him.

"I've got it."

"You sure?" he asks, one foot already on the ground and the other leg already swinging around. "I don't mind helping."

"I'm sure you don't," I mutter to myself, but I refuse to owe him another damn thing. "I'm sure. Thank you for the escort home."

He nods, cranks up his bike, gives me one last look, and then, thankfully, he rides away.

I'm near tears before I can manage to get the front door unlocked for Harley and the screen door back in place. I wouldn't be surprised if I come back out in a few hours to go to work and the thing is lying in the street. No doubt the landlord will blame me and I'll get billed for it. The guy is a complete asshole and constantly finds ways to shove his expenses off on me.

My chest threatens to cave in when I step inside and Harley is standing there with tears staining his little cheeks. "I'm sorry, Momma."

"Baby," I whisper, dropping my purse and the *Thank You* bag with our to-go containers in it. "What's wrong?"

"I forgot about the door, and now it's broken."

"Sweet boy." I draw him to my chest. "The door was already broken."

"I made it worse."

"The wind made it worse."

He sniffles some more, and I feel the burn of my own tears threaten. I promise myself five minutes to cry after I put him to bed. I feel his tiny shoulders shake with sobs, and it's only after the vow of ten minutes of crying that I get myself under control enough to hold him at arm's length and look down at him with a smile.

"I thought you were going to do tattoos? You can't do tattoos if you're crying."

"You'll still let me have them even though I broke the door?"

"You didn't break the door." I wipe away more tears. "The wind did. I can't wait to see how you look with tattoos, but no real ones until you're much older."

We spend twenty minutes applying tattoos to his stomach because I'll be damned if I will allow him to put them anywhere staff at the school would see them. The last thing we need is more conversation about how trashy we are despite other kids doing the very same things.

Since today was payday and I was able to get some grocery shopping done amongst the craziness of Black Friday, we settle on the sofa for a quick snack before his bedtime.

"You're not going to eat those?" I ask, noticing two of the four cookies still left on the coffee table.

"I'm saving them," Harley says, never pulling his eyes from the movie.

"For when?"

"Tomorrow."

"We have more cookies for tomorrow."

He shrugs, and I know what he's doing. We don't always have cookies or juice. Some days, we have meatless dinners. Many families do that. Some families do it to save money or to cut back on calories, and it's healthy and they're commended for it. The only difference is, when you do it because there aren't cookies, juice, or meat in the house and there won't be until payday, then it's pitiful, it's deprivation, it's abuse, it's bad parenting.

He wants to ration the things we don't always have so he can fill in the void on those days.

I open my mouth to tell him to eat the cookies, that I'll find a way to make sure we have more, but that may be a promise I won't be able to keep. I pride myself on not lying to him, or at least keeping my lies to a minimum.

"We have our park day tomorrow," I tell him instead. "Better eat them now so you have the energy to run and play."

I may actually have the ability to keep snacks in the house between paychecks this time since Micah paid for dinner today. The happiness that will bring Harley makes me dislike him a little less, and then I feel guilty for disliking a stranger for no reason.

He wasn't suggestive at all today or at the gas station when we first met. He was honestly a breath of fresh air after the disgusting things those other guys said, and I was grateful for the distraction he provided to Harley because I knew a hundred questions would come from my kid after he heard some new words today. He asked Micah those questions instead, but knowing my child, he'll get around to asking those things to me, eventually.

I smile when his tiny hand reaches out to take another cookie from the table.

"Can we watch another movie after this?"

"Aren't you tired?"

He yawns. "Nope, and I don't have school tomorrow."

"You can stay up until I have to go to work," I tell him. "Mind if I take a nap?"

He shakes his head. I set an alarm on my phone, but find it difficult to fall asleep. When I close my eyes, I see dark beards, piercing blue eyes, and quick, genuine smiles. I hear the rumble of motorcycles and husky laughter. I feel warm, work-worn hands on my skin, soft lips on my neck, promises whispered in my ear.

I wake with my alarm going off, the television dark, and Harley curled up in front of me on the sofa, asleep.

I shift out from behind him and get ready for work, waiting until the very last minute to wake him. I have to help him into his jacket and shoes before walking him next door to Mrs. Greene's house. The sweet old lady next door knows better than most what it's like to be a single mother. She raised six kids after her husband took off when her youngest was three. She watches Harley at night, refusing to take money from me because and I quote, "he just sleeps."

In turn, I take care of her yard, pick up her prescriptions, and do her grocery shopping. I'd do more if she'd let me, but she's as stubborn as I am if not more.

I unlock her front door with the key she gave me, kiss Harley on the forehead as he settles down on her sofa, and make sure to lock the door on my way out.

Working for an overnight cleaning service isn't going to make me rich, but it's honest work. There are a lot of people that can't find a job, so I make sure to be on time every day and work hard. At least being unemployed right now isn't something I'll have to worry about.

Chapter 4

Snake

Showing up at a woman's house when you don't know her last name probably isn't smart. Showing up at nine in the morning on a Saturday? Even less smart. Not realizing the woman could be married or have a live-in boyfriend until you arrive? Pure ignorance.

It doesn't stop me from getting out of the truck because let's face it, if she does have a man, he's not a very good one. That screen door nearly flew away last night, and that was over twelve hours ago. She did a good job of propping it up I noticed when I drove by again last night, but now it's just sort of hanging there. If she had a man, it should be fixed. The damn hardware store opened an hour and a half ago. That's plenty of time to go and get a new damn door and get it fixed. Hopefully, I'm getting pissed about a man that doesn't exist, because I want to be the man to fix her shit when it breaks.

I don't pull anything from the truck before I walk up her empty driveway. Her car isn't here, but that doesn't mean some deadbeat isn't inside. I knock on the door gently, but no one answers. I knock a little louder a second time, and it goes unanswered again.

So, I get to work.

I pull out my tools, first removing the frame of the old screen door. The thing is mostly rust anyway. I toss the thing in the back of the truck and pull out the new one.

I noticed the old woman standing on her porch when I first pulled up, but as I carry the new screen door up the driveway, it seems she's settled in for a show because she's got a cup of coffee in her hand and a warm jacket over her long nightgown. I give her a nod.

Hanging the new screen door isn't hard as much as it is bulky. I could've asked one of the other guys to come help me, but they went to *Jake's* last night and didn't get in until early this morning. Besides, I want to be the only one who gets credit for this. Not that I expect anything in return.

I can feel the neighbor's eyes boring into my back as I work, but I wait until I'm nearly finished before acknowledging her.

"Does it look straight?" I ask without looking at her.

"Seems so," she says, her voice sounding stronger than I would've given her credit for.

I turn, finding her right behind me on the stoop rather than across the yard on her own porch. She cocks an eyebrow at the shock on my face.

"That old one was nearly rusted through."

"What's Brinson paying to have this fixed?"

"Brinson?" I ask, wondering if that is Lucy's last name.

"The landlord," the old woman explains.

"I'm doing this for Lucy," I correct.

"I need some things done around my place," she hints, and I just love how forward elderly people are.

"Lucy is a friend." Well, I'd like Lucy to be a friend. "But I can give you the number of a guy in town. He does great work, honest prices, great turn around, and incredible work ethic."

"Is he as good looking as you are?"

I huff a laugh.

She sips her coffee, waiting for an answer.

"I'll make sure Lucy gets his information to you."

"You do that, dear," she says as she turns around and shuffles back to her porch.

I'm putting tools back in the truck when Lucy's car pulls into the driveway. Lucy is wary of me standing by the truck, but Harley bounds out of the backseat with a wide smile on his face.

"Micah! We went to the park!"

"Did you have fun?"

"I was the fastest on the slide!"

"I bet you were."

He runs up to me, stopping near my legs with only inches to spare.

"Are you here to see Momma?"

I look up at Lucy who is standing near her car.

"I had a spare screen door at the clubhouse, and I noticed you guys needed a new one."

Lucy looks from me to the new door on the front of her house. Her face falls.

"I broke the old one yesterday."

"The wind broke it," I tell him. "I saw the whole thing. It was pretty rusty."

Harley runs up on to the porch to check the new screen door out like it's a toy as I close some of the distance between his mother and me. She opens her purse.

"How much do I owe you?"

"Nothing," I tell her, shoving my hands into my pockets, making it clear I won't accept a penny from her.

"And I'm just supposed to believe you had one lying around that fit perfectly."

I shrug.

"Momma, can we have hot chocolate?"

"Yes," she says to him before turning back to me.

Her eyes search mine as if she expects me to say something. If I met her at the bar, I might make a suggestion. I might flirt and ask her to spend a little time with me. If I knew her expectations were to get my leather cut off my shoulders and my jeans around my ankles, I'd pounce on this woman in a heartbeat, but that's not where she's at. Lucy is nothing like the women I meet at *Jake's* or the women that used to come around the clubhouse looking for a good time.

She's exhausted, and it's clear in the shadows under her eyes and the slight droop in her shoulders.

"Do you like hot chocolate?"

"Love it," I tell her. "But you don't owe me anything, Lucy. You needed a screen door. I had one. I didn't do it to get something in return. That's not how I operate. Now, your neighbor. I think she wants me to do some work for her, and with the way she was talking, I wouldn't put it past her to ask me to do it in just my boxers."

Lucy chuckles, and the sound of it hits me in the gut.

"Mrs. Greene is harmless. Mostly." She looks at the front porch, smiling as Harley grabs his soccer ball from the porch and runs toward us. "Stay in the yard and I'll make hot chocolate."

She looks at me one last time before walking away, and I kind of like that she doesn't invite me in. She's cautious, and she should be, especially with having a young child. She's protecting her space.

"Do you play soccer?"

"I don't," I answer honestly. "Can you teach me?"

"I'm not very good, but we can kick the ball back and forth."

We stand about fifteen feet away from each other because her yard isn't very big and kick the ball back and forth.

"Did you guys not sleep very well last night?"

"Momma doesn't sleep at night."

"No?" I ask as I tap the ball with the tip of my boot back in his direction.

"Momma works nights. I sleep on Mrs. Greene's couch. We go to the park on Saturday morning. She has the weekends off."

"Nights? At that gas station out on the highway?"

There aren't many places in town that stay open all night long, but there are a few occupations in town that would keep a woman up at night. I don't want my mind going there, but some women have to do what they have to do to take care of their families.

"She cleans office buildings. She can't work during the day because the business-people are there," he says with a grunt as he kicks the ball with all his might.

"Ah, ok." Relief washes over me as I tell myself I won't look into her, but I know I will.

She seems like a decent woman, and I know most people wouldn't tell their kids what they really do for a living. It would flatten me to know she's selling herself to make ends meet.

"Yours is on the kitchen table," Lucy says as she walks out onto the small porch with a steaming mug in her hand.

Harley scoops up the ball, depositing it on the porch before heading inside.

"Thank you," I tell her when she offers me the mug.

I take a seat on the top step as she leans against one of the banisters.

"Harley says you work nights. That's got to be tough."

"I think Sure Clean has been one of the best things to happen for me," she says. "I can sleep while he's at school. We get the afternoons together. Mrs. Greene watches him at night while I work. I'm just happy to have a job. There are a lot of single moms that don't."

And she just answered my question about a spouse or boyfriend. I nod and take a sip of the hot chocolate.

"What do you do for a living?"

"I work for Cerberus."

"The motorcycle club?"

"Yeah. Heard of us?"

She shakes her head. "I've lived here for a couple of years, so I guess I probably should have. I've seen guys on bikes, but I haven't paid much attention. I keep to myself, don't ask questions. Do you guys own like a shop or something?"

I chuckle. "Watch a lot of TV?"

She shakes her head. "We watch a lot of cartoons, but you'd be surprised just how lacking kids' entertainment is on motorcycle diversity."

"Such a shame," I tell her with a smile. "We actually travel a lot. I can't really go into what we do, but it's all good stuff. We help people. We're the good guys."

"And you were in the Marine Corps?"

"Eight years. All of us were in the Corps, actually. It's a requirement for Cerberus."

"And that makes you how old?"

"Thirty-one."

"You seem older."

"Wow." I laugh.

"Sorry. I don't mean it in a bad way, just that you're mature. I knew bikers before, and they're—"

"Wild? Like they'll never grow up?"

She nods.

"We all have our moments. We see a lot of bad stuff, so we like to have fun when we can, but we know when to be serious."

"I'm sorry for the millions of questions. I know Harley asked you so many yesterday."

I look up at her, cup close to my mouth so she can't see just how wide my smile is. "I'm an open book, Lucy."

"I'm twenty-eight. Harley is six. He's in first grade."

"And his dad?"

She cringes, and I open my mouth to tell her never mind. I don't want the conversation to stop. I'll talk about myself all damn day if it keeps her from shutting down and asking me to leave.

"Prison."

Damn it. That can't be easy on either of them.

"He messed up when he was young. A lot, and often." She shakes her head as if looking back now, she can't believe that she ever got tangled up in that situation. "I wasn't an innocent angel in all of it. I made mistakes, too. He got caught. I didn't. I grew up quicker. We split before I got pregnant with Harley, but you know how exes go. Sometimes bad choices come crawling back, and more mistakes are made. Well, I wouldn't say mistakes because I wouldn't have Harley, and I love my son. But Robbie was a mistake. We both know that now."

"Does Harley ever see his dad?"

A small smile tugs at her mouth as she looks out across the yard. "I take him to Santa Fe once a month for visitation. It's as much a part of his life he can be other than letters in the mail. He was never a bad guy. He had a hard life growing up. I'm not making excuses for the man, but he's gotten better in prison. He's gotten his GED. He's staying out of trouble."

"You guys planning on making it work when he's released?"

She scoffs, her head shaking. "Not a chance. There was nothing there between Robbie and me. Once we were both clean and the highs wore off, neither of us could figure out how we connected in the first place. We aren't compatible at all. We'll always be in each other's lives because of Harley, but there are no romantic inclinations at all."

That's good news.

"And Robbie knows this?"

She looks down at me, and I make sure to meet her eyes. The woman has to know that I'm interested, but just in case, I don't want any trouble from the man. He could easily be biding his time, telling her what she wants to hear before he's released and gets out, ready to stake his claim once again.

"That ship sailed a long time ago."

"When is he due to get released?"

"Soon. Like in the next six months or so, but he has family in Las Cruces, so that's where he'll likely end up."

She mentioned being in Robbie's life because of Harley, but does that mean they're going to be near each other? Does that mean she goes where he goes or that Robbie stays around here? It may be a little soon to ask these questions.

"Do you date?"

She's silent a little too long, so I have to look back up at her.

She's staring down at me.

"Do you?"

She huffs a humorless laugh.

"No. I'm a mom."

"Moms date," I argue.

"I tried dating several years ago, but my responsibilities are to my child." She shakes her head as if she's trying to rid it of bad memories. "Men aren't interested in the real shit that comes along with dating a woman with a kid."

I hate that she's had bad experiences, but at the same time, I'm glad she hasn't met someone worth keeping.

I stand, handing her back the empty coffee mug. "You just haven't met a real man yet."

I wink at her before walking back to my truck.

Chapter 5

Lucy

"After this, I have to take a nap," I tell Harley as I pull the popcorn from the microwave.

"It's Sunday," he says, his little eyebrows dipping together from his frown.

"I picked up an extra shift."

I won't explain that it's getting closer to Christmas because I don't want to get his hopes up about extra presents. He could get sick, and I may have to use the extra money for a visit to the doctor's office, or I could have a flat tire and need to get one replaced. Any number of things could happen between now and then, but I never turn down an extra shift. They don't happen very often because all the ladies I work with need every hour they can manage.

"Don't pout," I tell him. "Get the movie started."

"Maybe we can play *Uno* instead."

I smile. "I'm not going to go easy on you."

He narrows his eyes. "You never do."

"Get the cards and get ready to get spanked."

He laughs, the best sound I could ever hear, as he scrambles to his room for the worn deck of cards. I pour the popcorn into a bowl and pour a cup of juice for him and a glass of water from the tap for me. By the time I'm setting everything on the kitchen table, he's there trying to shuffle the cards with his tiny hands. He can't quite manage it, but I don't step in. He hates it when he's made to feel as if he's not big enough to do something. I sit back, snacking on buttered popcorn and wait for him to either consider them shuffled enough or for him to ask for help.

"Are you going to go on a date with Micah?"

"What did I tell you about listening in on adult conversations?"

He shrugs. We had this conversation last year when he was being nosy during a conversation I had with Mrs. Greene after overhearing one of the other parents trash talking me at the end-of-the-year awards ceremony. I was ready to show the other mom just how trailer trash I was, and she was talking me off the ledge. Harley didn't take hearing it very well and shoved that parent's kid at the park that summer when he saw them a few weeks later.

"I like him," Harley says as he passes out the *Uno* cards.

"Because he has a motorcycle."

"Because he doesn't pretend like I don't exist, and he doesn't say nasty things in front of me."

Man, if he brings up what those men were saying Friday evening at the diner, I may track those guys down myself and set them on fire.

"Well, Micah didn't give me his number or ask me for mine, so I don't know if he'll go out on a date with me."

"I just want you to know you have my permission."

I try my best to hide my smile. "Oh, do I?"

He nods. "Is that seven? Count yours? I think I dealt too many."

"It's seven. How many do you have?"

"Seven."

"Okay, let's play."

We play hand after hand after hand until the popcorn is gone. I don't let the child win. I don't have to. He has a pretty decent strategy for a six-year-old. He wins more than he loses, and he's quite content to curl up on the sofa to watch a movie when it's time for me to get a couple of hours of sleep before my shift tonight.

I press a kiss to his forehead before turning toward my bedroom.

"Don't—"

"Open the door if anyone knocks. I got it, Momma. I'm not a baby. Don't turn on the oven or use the microwave."

"You're the best kid I've ever had."

"I'm the only kid you've ever had," he says with a huge smile.

I crawl in between my sheets, used to the scratchy fabric, and sink into the mattress. I'm exhausted, but it's nothing new. I'm always tired. Stress keeps me from sleeping. I worry about everything, and the problem is, I don't ever envision a future where I don't have to worry about tomorrow or next month's bills or living paycheck to paycheck. That kind of life just isn't in the plans for me.

The alarm on my phone goes off, and I catch it early, the vibration under my pillow waking me before the musical tone has the chance to get very loud, but then I stiffen because I hear voices. They aren't the familiar sounds of the movies Harley watches on repeat. We don't have cable or Netflix because we can't afford such luxuries. We're relegated to DVDs we're able to score at garage sales.

I rush into the living room to find Harley leaning into the open front window.

"What are you doing?" I hiss.

"You said don't open the door!" Harley says as he spins around to face me.

The boy is proud of his work around the rule, a wide grin on his face, cheeks rosy from the cool air.

And there's Micah, the man also has a wide smile on his face. His eyes dip before they meet mine again, making me realize I'm wearing a tank top, sleep shorts and socks. That's literally it.

"Shit! I mean, shit! I mean, crap! Shoot! Sorry!" I grab the lap blanket off the couch and toss it around my shoulders, wrapping it around myself. I don't know why I bother. It's not like the man didn't just see my peaked nipples.

"That's three quarters in the swear jar."

"It was my fault," Micah says with a wide grin as he leans to the side.

I swear I hear him whisper, "But so worth it."

"Go put this in the jar, little man."

Micah hands over change to my son who takes it with a smile before bounding away to the kitchen.

"Are you sitting on the front porch?"

I step closer, but his eyes don't inch higher. They're locked on my legs. Why do I like it so much? "Yeah. Umm. He said you were sleeping, and I didn't want to talk very loud."

"I picked up an extra shift tonight. I needed a nap."

I crouch down, so he has to meet my eyes.

"I told him you wanted his number, so I got it for you."

Harley shoves a slip of paper in front of my face, and Micah grins. "Heck of a wingman you have there."

"I didn't... that's not how the conversation went."

His teeth dig into his lower lip, his blue eyes sparkling as he watches me.

"There's a tree lighting in the park next Saturday. It's a community thing, so it doesn't have to really be a date since you don't do that sort of thing. We could ride together. You know to save gas."

I get the feeling he isn't trying to make fun of me at all, but he's wanting to take me out while still staying within the parameters I've set.

"I spend Saturdays with Harley."

"I wouldn't take you out without him, Lucy. I know you two are a package deal. It's gonna be cold, so make sure you dress warm." His eyes skate over me one more time. "If you wear that, I'll be tempted to warm you up myself."

That's probably the very first thing he's said to me that has had any form of innuendo to it, and it landed exactly where it was intended. I have to look over my shoulder to see where Harley is at in the room, and I breathe a sigh of relief to find him enthralled with something on the television.

I don't want to have to explain why Micah would even think I'd wear my pajamas out of the house or how he would warm me up, but I come up with several ways he could as I get dressed for work.

I realize just how good of a wingman my son is when I get a text thirty minutes later.

See you Saturday evening 7pm. Wear something warm.

I find myself smiling all night at work.

Chapter 6

Snake

"Texting again?" Ace asks as he settles in the chair beside me in the garage.

I nod, my face angled down at my phone.

"She only gets thirty minutes for lunch."

"Then shouldn't you let the woman eat?"

My nose scrunches up with his words because he has a point. I've been bothering her all damn week during her lunch break.

"Leave him alone," Skid interrupts. "The woman can text as she chews. She has a kid. I'm sure she's good at multitasking."

It only alleviates the guilt a little.

Me: Are you eating?

I watch the three little dots as they appear on the screen.

Lucy: Peanut butter and jelly today.

I smile down at my phone.

Me: Grape or strawberry?

Lucy: Strawberry of course. It's the best.

Me: Creamy or chunky?

Lucy: Creamy.

Me: You'd tell me if I'm bothering you, right?

Lucy: Yes. I like having an adult to talk to.

Me: You don't talk with the people you work with?

Lucy: They complain a lot. I don't like being in the middle of people's drama.

Me: Understandable.

"You really like this girl, huh?" Ace asks, kicking at my boot with his own.

I look up at my best friend.

"There's just something about her."

"She's hot," Skid says.

I nod in agreement. "That she is.

"There are always hot chicks," Ace adds. "What's different about her?"

I shrug. "Couldn't tell you."

"Is it the damsel in distress thing?"

I shake my head. "She's doing fine on her own. I mean, she struggles, but most single moms do. She's handling her business. She seems like a good mom. Harley is a great kid. He's respectful, well taken care of. She doesn't need a man. She was agitated when I bought their dinner the other day, not expectant at all. She wanted to pay for the screen door I replaced. Wouldn't even invite me inside. She's cautious."

"So now she's a challenge?" Skid asks, leaning forward in his chair like he feels the need to defend her in some way.

This is what I love about my friends. We've never had a problem getting women, and we're quick to accept an offer from a woman who's wanting to play but coercing a woman into bed isn't our thing. We don't play games or manipulate, and both of these guys would be on my ass if they thought that's what I was doing.

"She's not a challenge," I assure him. "She's different."

"Love different?" Skid raises an eyebrow, a small smile playing on his lips.

I grin a little too. "I don't know, man. It's early days, but she's special. I can just feel it."

"Dating a woman with a kid isn't the same as dating a single woman. Package deals have to be treated with a softer touch," Ace warns.

"I'm well aware," I grumble. "I'm not playing games with her. I'm taking both of them to the tree lighting on Saturday. I'm not alienating the kid to get to his mom."

"Good," Skid says as he leans back in his seat.

"So does this mean you aren't going to *Jake's* with us after the tree lighting?"

"Not a chance," I tell him.

"Pussy-whipped already," Skid says.

***

"Nice truck!" Harley says as he waits for Lucy to situate the booster seat from her car.

"Thanks, little man. I didn't think to grab one of those," I tell her.

"It's fine. I don't expect people without kids to have one. Honestly, it would be weird if you did. There you go. Seat belt," she says.

Harley, filled with energy, plops in the seat and reaches for the belt. His little body is thrumming with excitement.

"We went last year. It was so cold. My new jacket is going to keep me warm this year!"

Lucy's eyes dart away, and I have no idea what the look means, so I ignore it.

"Hopefully, there will be a vendor selling hot chocolate, but I doubt it'll be as good as your mom's."

"No one's hot chocolate is as good as mom's," Harley says as Lucy gets in the passenger seat.

I wait for her to buckle up before closing her door and walking around to the driver's side.

The drive to the main street in town is quiet, the roads already crowded by the time we arrive.

"I need you to stay close," Lucy says in warning as I try to find a place to park. "No running off."

"Okay, Momma." His nose is plastered to the window, his eyes wide as he takes everything in.

Before turning off the truck, I look to the back seat at Harley. I don't have kids, and I never dated a woman with one before, but I already feel protective of him.

"It's really crowded here tonight," I say to him. He turns to face me, nodding as I speak. "I don't want you to get hurt or lost, but I do want you to have fun. We're going to spend time doing all that you want to do, but we have to do it at old man speed, okay?"

He nods with a grin. "Okay."

I nod; he nods. We understand each other. Lucy chuckles.

"Wait for me," I tell her, turning off the truck and climbing out.

I circle the vehicle and offer my hand to help her down. Doing this is two-fold. One, I want to help her, and two, once I have her hand, I don't plan to let her go. She said she doesn't date, but that's exactly what this is. I keep my hand in hers as I open the door for Harley, offering my other to him.

He releases mine once his feet are on the ground, but I drop my fingers to his shoulder, stopping him before he can bound away.

"Mine or your momma's."

He takes Lucy's hand before we head toward the center of town.

Christmas music plays, and despite the lack of snow on the ground, the air is cold enough to put everyone in a festive mood. Kids run about, not being as disciplined as Harley. People smile and laugh as the scent of fried foods and coffee fill the air.

Lucy watches the delight in Harley's eyes, and I watch her. She is so damned beautiful, just absolutely gorgeous.

We walk around, and I follow her lead. If Harley wants something, I wait for her response. If she looks like she's going to reach for her purse, I buy it. If she shakes her head, I don't offer. I'm not going to go against her wishes. I want to make things easier for her, but at the same time, I'm not trying to buy either of their affection. It's a fine line because I want to give both of them the world. Dropping a couple hundred dollars tonight isn't a big deal, but it can be just what will make her tell me to stay away forever when I drop her off tonight.

Harley ends up with an elf hat, huge ears included, and a hot chocolate with too many marshmallows. I opt for a black coffee. Lucy sips on a peppermint tea while we wait for the lighting ceremony to begin, and in true Farmington fashion, the switch is flipped, and the entire town goes black.

I hold Lucy closer, making sure her arms are around Harley, and I wait, ears wide open and assessing the night for danger before the kinks are worked out and everything is relit.

Everyone gasps at the pretty lights, and it takes several long moments before my heart rate returns to normal. I'm not a stranger to adrenaline rushes. I get them every time we take on a new job, but I've never felt like I had so much to lose before.

"That was exciting and dramatic," Lucy says, a wide smile on her face.

"Very." I look down at her. She has no clue that the blackout wasn't intentional. All I can think is that there's a good chance bad people used it to their advantage, and I pray we don't wake up in the morning to reports of someone getting hurt or a child getting abducted during that two-minute period of blackness. Criminals use shit like that to their advantage, always looking for other people to slip up and make mistakes so they can benefit. "Do you want to walk around some more?"

Lucy looks from me down to Harley. He's rubbing his eyes, a tiny yawn escaping his lips.

"I think he's about ready to go. He was so excited all day, I think he wore himself out before you arrived."

Reluctant to back away and only touch her hand when so much of her is pulled against my body, I wait just a few seconds longer before nodding.

"How about a ride?" I ask Harley.

He looks up at me confused.

"Up here?" I ask, pointing to my shoulders.

His eyes widen as if he's never done it before, then I realize he probably hasn't. If his father has been in prison all of his life, and Lucy hasn't dated, then he's never had a male role model in his life. Lucy hasn't mentioned her parents, so there's a good chance he doesn't have a grandfather around much either.

"Is that okay?" I ask Lucy. "I should've asked before I offered."

She smiles before looking down at Harley. "Only if you're careful and don't bump your head on the moon."

Harley scoffs. "Mom, that's not possible. The moon is too far away."

He holds his arms up to me, and I don't waste a second lifting him to my shoulders. He grips my hair like he's terrified he's going to fall off. His squeals of happiness draw several eyes in our direction, but to those around us, we're just another happy family enjoying our evening. I'm not wearing my Cerberus cut because I didn't want her to feel uncomfortable. She already has this preconceived notion about bikers as it is. Ace and Skid are around here somewhere because according to them, the tree lighting ceremony is a better place to pick up women than the grocery store. If I needed them tonight, they would be around.

Lucy helps Harley into the back of the truck, and I resist the urge to help her into the passenger seat because she's perfectly capable. The little guy is asleep by the time we make it back to her house, but I don't offer to carry him inside. I do, however, unlock her door for her and hold the keys on her front porch until she gets him settled in his bed and returns.

"Thank you," she says as she rejoins me. "I had a lot of fun tonight."

"You're very welcome."

I'm mostly a gentleman, but holding this woman's hand all night, seeing the way she smiled up at me, I don't know that I can leave without pressing my lips to hers. She seems a little nervous, but not in a way that tells me she wants to escape.

She's not inching away or trying to put distance between us. She isn't holding onto the screen door. Hell, the thing is completely closed.

"I'm going to kiss you, Lucy."

She nibbles the corner of her lower lip, eyes blinking up at me as I lower my mouth. My fingers grip the coarse fabric of her jacket as I pull her closer to me. Her lips are warm, spiced with the mint of the tea she was drinking earlier, and I find myself starved for more.

She melts into me, her body angled as she trusts me with nearly the full weight of it.

My entire being is a live wire the second my tongue meets hers, and all those declarations of being a gentleman don't fade away. They disappear in a snap. Gone. Poof. Nonexistent.

Sharp breaths, what I would consider a gasp if they were made from her lips, not her nose, escape, and I know she's just as into it as I am. I pull back because if I don't, I won't have the power to stop.

I press my lips to hers, soft, gentle kisses three more times, loving that after just one kiss, her lips are cherry red and a little swollen. God, what will they look like after I've gone after her for hours?

"I want to see you again," I whisper, my mouth mere inches from hers.

"We don't have plans tomorrow, and Monday, Harley will be at school. I don't have work until that evening."

Jesus, I know exactly what she's saying.

"Want to see me both days?"

She nods.

"Pizza and movies tomorrow?"

"That sounds perfect."

"See you then, beautiful." I press my lips to hers once more before taking a step back.

God, I want to follow her inside the house and spend the rest of the night with her in my arms, but I know that's moving too fast. I'll get to see her tomorrow and then the day after. That's just going to have to be good enough.

Chapter 7

Lucy

I have great days with Harley. I've learned to count my blessings. Although I don't have a lot of money, we have fun when we can. We go to the park and play games. We spend time watching movies. We have cheap fun.

Micah showed up yesterday with a pile of pizzas and a stack of animated movies. I don't know if Harley told him we don't have cable, but the man came prepared.

We spent the day on the couch laughing so much I woke this morning with my stomach a little sore. It was an amazing day, and I can't seem to wipe the smile from my face. Micah paid a ton of attention to Harley while holding my hand the entire day. I didn't feel left out at all. I sort of loved that he focused on my son because I knew what I promised. I knew my day was today, and I didn't get much sleep last night after he left with that promise floating around in my head.

After sending Harley to school this morning on the bus, I flew around the house getting ready, his whispered promises in my ears.

He was appropriate yesterday, keeping a casual distance between us the whole day—a different man than the one that kissed me like he wanted to crawl inside of me the night before on the porch. He kissed me much the same yesterday evening before leaving, but while he was here and in Harley's presence, he was a complete gentleman. I love the dichotomy of it, that he knows who I need him to be and when.

It also sends a thrill up my spine as I wait for him to arrive today because I know who I'm going to get once he arrives.

I shake my hands out as I pace the floor, praying my deodorant does its job because I'm incredibly nervous. I'm also wondering if we're moving too fast. Micah is unlike any man I've ever met, and I'm second-guessing myself.

Am I attracted to him because he's simply saying the right things and acting the right way? He's the first man to come into our lives that's acted like a decent human being. The first person to acknowledge the importance of me being a mother first. I want to believe it isn't all an act, but I guess only time will tell.

I'm attracted to him as I suspect many women are. He's ridiculously handsome and kind. Not once have I caught him looking at Harley like he wishes he'd just disappear so he could get me alone, and believe me, I've been waiting to catch him do just that. Men say a lot of things and then get caught acting differently.

I catch sight of myself in the mirror hanging on the living room wall, and I see some of that guilt I can't manage to fully let go of. Maybe it's a mom thing. Harley likes him, and that makes me happy, but I don't want to be *too* happy. I don't want to lose sight of what's most important. I don't want to get lost in a man and make bad decisions. I did that with Robbie and my life went off the rails.

Maybe this is just a little fun. No one said it had to be serious, but if that's the case, then I've already made the mistake of letting Harley get close. He asked last night after his bath when Micah was coming back over. Of course, I didn't mention that he was coming to see me today. I wasn't about to explain why he'd visit me alone in the middle of the day. I find myself frowning at the thought of whatever this is with him not going anywhere because I really like this guy.

I don't have any more time to worry about it because the roar of his motorcycle filters in from the street, and that same anticipation that kept me from sleeping last night ramps back up to full force.

I resist the urge to open the door and meet him on the porch. I'm eager, but I don't want to come across as too anxious. I can't seem to get my trembling hands on the same page.

The motorcycle engine stops, and the silence is deafening. The pause between as I wait for the sound of his boots on my front porch as anticipatory as that three-minute wait after taking that first pregnancy test. Although I was expecting it, I still jolt when the knock comes.

"Hi," I whisper shyly when I open the door.

The man is huge, his leather-clad bearded body taking up nearly the entire doorway as he smiles down at me.

"Mornin', sweetheart."

He doesn't advance on me. His eyes skate up and down my body, and I wonder exactly how he sees my leggings and over-sized sweater. I'm not wearing shoes, only fuzzy socks. I didn't want to look like I was trying too hard, and I knew we weren't leaving the house.

"You going to stand out there all day?"

"You going to invite me in?" he challenges, his blue eyes sparkling with humor.

"What happens when you get in here?"

"Anything you want."

"Harley has *Uno*."

He grins.

"Or we could take a nap."

His smile grows. "I'm a great cuddler."

"Yeah?"

"Only one condition. I have to be the big spoon."

"Of course," I tell him.

"And I can't nap in jeans."

"I'd want you to be comfortable."

"I go commando."

I grin. "I do, too."

His eyes drop to the apex of my thighs.

"My jeans are really uncomfortable right now, sweetheart." His right hand comes down and adjusts the front of his jeans, and there's something seriously sexy with the sight of him doing that in riding leathers, that area framed by them as if keeping it on display.

"You should come inside and take them off." I step to the side and hold the door open wider.

He doesn't waste a second stepping inside my house. Nor does he miss a beat wrapping his arm around me and lowering his mouth to mine. The restrained man that was here last night isn't the same man that enters today. One hand is on my ass. The other shoves the doors closed and flips the lock into place.

I feel silly when he lifts me off my feet, but that doesn't stop me from wrapping my legs around his waist as he carries me to my room. He doesn't have to ask where it is. There are only three doors down the short hallway and since he used the restroom yesterday and Harley's door is always open, it's a simple deduction.

My room is plain, the sheets and comforter bought on clearance from the Dollar Store. Decorations are minimal, but I get the feeling this man isn't worried about any of it, and even if he were, he's not the type to worry about things like that.

"You're so overdressed," I mutter against his mouth, my fingers unable to reach the zipper on his freezing cold leather jacket.

"It's cold outside." His lips are on my neck, his beard abrading my skin in the best way. "Don't want to put you down."

"Just for a minute. Let me help."

I wiggle until he releases me, chuckling when he looks desolate at not having his hands on me.

"It's like opening an early Christmas present," I say as I reach for the zipper on his jacket. "Just stand there and let me unwrap you."

"It would be easier if you were already naked," he teased, and I take a step back and look up at him.

"Really? You'd be able to keep your hands off me?"

"Yes."

"Liar." I smack at his chest, but he's wearing so many layers, I doubt he felt it.

"What about a compromise? Just the leggings?"

"I'm not wearing anything under them," I remind him.

He groans, his head rolling back until he's looking up at the ceiling.

"Don't turn into a baby."

I push the jacket off his shoulders, but he catches it before it hits the ground.

"Never on the floor," he says. "Not when my cut is with it."

There's no anger in his tone, just an educational lesson. He steps to the side, laying it across the top of my dresser before stepping in front of me once again. My fingers trace the muscles of his chest on top of his thermal.

"You're supposed to be unwrapping me."

"I'm savoring."

"I have no patience. Keep that in mind when it's my turn, okay?"

I nod, but really my attention is on the hard plains under my hands as I lift the hem of his shirt.

"So much hair," I say in awe.

"I'm a man, sweetheart."

"Yes, you are," I whisper, swallowing hard. "Hold this."

He lifts his hand in time to clutch the shirt as my fingers wander over his abdomen. The muscles bunch and flex with my attention.

"You're killing me, Lucy. Can I take this off?"

I nod, my eyes still glued to his stomach, but I take a step back as he pulls the shirt over his head, getting a good look at his full torso as it's revealed. His smile is a little shy.

"Are you objectifying me?"

I nod. "Can't help it. You're perfect."

"My cock is big, too."

My eyes lift to his, but the humor is gone. The lighter blue tones have turned darker, needier.

"Do your boots have to be unlaced or can they be pulled or kicked off?"

"I can kick them off."

"Do that."

I stay back while he works his boots off, pulling my sweater over my head.

"You're cheating," he says when I drop it to the floor. "I'm supposed to unwrap you."

"I can put it back on." I bend to reach for the sweater.

"Don't you dare."

I give him a grin as he reaches for the belt of his riding leathers, working it open before he opens the button and zipper of his jeans. The head of his cock pops out of the top as if the thing has been trying for hours to seek relief. I can't seem to pull my eyes from it.

"Lucy? Eyes up here, sweetheart."

Guiltily, I snap my eyes back up to his, doing my best to keep them there even as he bends a little to kick the rest of his clothes off.

"I want to do everything under the sun to you today."

"I want that, too," I tell him.

"I want to taste your sweet pussy."

I nod because that sounds amazing. If the man does that as well as he kisses, then I'm in for a special treat.

"I want your mouth on my cock."

"Okay." I start to lower to my knees, but he shakes his head.

"But the first time either of us come, it's going to be with me buried to my balls inside of you."

I drop my eyes to his waist. "I don't know if that's going to be possible."

He laughs. "Oh, sweetheart. It's possible. You're so wet for me already."

"How would you—"

His eyes drop between my legs, and it's like the glance made me aware of my body. I know what I'm going to find before I even look, but that doesn't stop me.

Wearing white leggings was a bad idea. Like wearing a white bathing suit then getting in the pool, my arousal has left literally nothing to the imagination. I'm soaking through, my lower lips on full display.

"Don't," he whispers when I try to cover myself. "That's the sexiest thing I've ever seen. Peel them down slowly, Lucy. I want to see them stick to you. That's it. Damn it, woman. What a pretty pussy."

I bite my lips as I do what he says. I've never felt sexier before in my life. I've had two sexual partners since Robbie, but those were quick, unsatisfactory romps not worth mentioning. Today is already ten times better and we haven't even touched each other besides kissing.

"I'm so sorry," he says, and I snap my eyes up at him.

"Wh-What?"

His eyes find mine, and I see a little disappointment in them.

"You have to work tonight." His head shakes a little. "You're going to be sore, sweetheart. I hate that you're going to be sore, but I'm going to spend the entire day inside of you. I won't be able to help it."

"You're sorry for that?" He nods, genuine guilt in his eyes.

"I promise lots of orgasms. You'll probably beg me to stop, and if you really mean it, just say like spaghetti or something."

"Okay," I agree, knowing I never will. I mean, is there such a thing as too many orgasms?

"And this, too," he says as he steps closer, his hands going around my back to unsnap my bra with a skill level I don't want to think about right now, or ever if I can help it. "Fuck, sweetheart. Just one little taste. Don't touch my cock."

In an effort to keep from doing just that, I wrap my arms around his neck as his expert tongue goes to work on my nipples. Jesus, I've never felt anything like it.

"Micah," I moan, and then I lose all sense of myself when his fingers slip between my legs, teasing my clit before two slide inside of me with no resistance.

I'm so ready for him, so gone for this man that I don't notice him lifting me and producing a condom from thin air until he's spreading me out on the bed and rolling it down his very eager erection.

"It's… umm, been awhile," I whisper.

"I've got you," he says as he lines up.

Before he shoves inside, he leans down close, his eyes locked on mine.

He watches me as he slides inside, his hand on the back of my neck as it arches with his intrusion.

"Fuck, baby, take me. Jesus, Lucy, that's my girl." His hips flex back before he moves forward again.

I can't seem to close my mouth. My jaw refuses to work the way it's supposed to.

"Micah," I pant. "Please."

I don't know what I'm asking for or what I need, but he must read minds because he shifts a little, lifting my leg a little higher on his hip, and it opens me perfectly. A husky sound comes from deep inside of him as his lips meet mine, his tongue sweeping inside of my mouth, and then I realize he kept his promise. He's all the way inside of me, our bodies meeting fully in the middle. I'm so full, and it's never been like this before. It's a full-body experience, the penetration, the brush of his chest hair on my skin, the grip of his fingers on my neck, his lips on mine.

With Robbie, we were bumbling teens, and even after gaining a little experience, we were either too high to remember what we'd done or I was never really into it and only did it to get him off my back. It was never an enjoyable experience. I'm two minutes into this with Micah and I can already feel that fluttering deep inside I've only experienced late at night when I'm in my room alone.

"You okay?" he asks as he lifts up a few inches, his thumb sweeping down my cheek.

I nod because I know if I speak, I may cry. I refuse to be the woman that gets sappy because she's experiencing great sex for the first time in her life.

"Make me come," I manage.

He grins with a roll of his hips. "I like where your head is at. Spread your legs, Lucy. Hold them up under your knees. Let me do all the work."

And boy does he work.

Micah gets up on his palms, hips snapping, and it takes mere minutes for that fluttering low in my belly to turn into an inferno in my gut. My eyes go blurry. My legs tremble. A thin layer of sweat covers my entire body despite the chilliness in the air.

"I'm—"

I don't even have time to say it before I implode.

"Goddamn it," he grunts. "Fuck, baby. Milk my cock."

Micah freezes inside of me, giving my body something to clench around, and it's spectacular. Just as I'm coming down, he starts all over again, hips working. He leans back, repositioning his legs so he's bent at the knees and my body is angled up.

His thumb on my clit is like a bolt of lightning, and he doesn't stop working me over until I come again. Only then does he let himself fall over the edge.

The man is absolute perfection when he orgasms, his eyes glassy and unfocused, his muscles taut and flexed, a sheen of sweat covering his abdomen.

What an experience. If this is only fun, I have to say it's the most fun I've ever had in my life.

He gets off the bed to dispose of the condom and get a bottle of water. He gives me half an hour before he tastes me like he promised. Forty-five minutes before his cock is in my throat, but it isn't until two in the afternoon that I finally have to whisper the word spaghetti.

Chapter 8

Snake

Maybe it was a little sneaky, but it's too late now.

During the time I spent between Lucy's legs, she confessed that Harley had trouble at school with some of the kids and the staff because she doesn't make a lot of money. Dominic's daughter goes to the same school, and she doesn't have any problems. Of course, they live in a nice house on the lake, so no one looks down on her. Harley doesn't have it so easy.

When she was blissed out on orgasms, I offered to pick him up from school, on the motorcycle of course, because I was thoughtful enough to buy him a helmet. With the promise of driving very slowly and bringing back an early dinner, she finally relented.

I hate that he's having trouble, but I know that it'll never change. They could win the lottery tomorrow, and he'll still be the kid that was once poor. The only way to overcome something like that is to be the new kid in a new school that has money, and that's not something that's going to be different for him and his mother.

I wait patiently outside the school, waving to a couple of the mothers that I recognize from the events we've done in the community. I made sure that Lucy called the school to let them know that I'd be the one picking Harley up, so I didn't catch any grief. I provided my driver's license when I first arrived, and now I just have to wait for him to walk out. I don't have to wait long, and like little ducks in a row behind his teacher, I spot Harley before he spots me because he's looking for his mother's car. Several kids notice the motorcycle before he does. They point and get excited, and I give him a wave. He doesn't run to me like most kids would. He waits for the teacher to give him permission, and it makes me wonder why he has trouble with the staff if he's always this well behaved. I guess it just goes to show that adults never really grow up either. What an unbelievable world we live in when grown-ups don't act like adults.

His smile grows wider with each step he takes.

"Hey there, little man," I tell him when he's right up beside me.

His mouth is hanging open, but then it suddenly falls, and his little chin begins to quiver.

"What happened to momma?"

"Nothing. She's fine. I promise. She said I could pick you up. Look what I got for you." I hold up the child-sized helmet.

His little eyes search mine, and I know he's searching them for the truth. It makes me wonder how many people in his short life have lied to him.

"Look," I say as I place my hand on his shoulder. "We'll call her, okay?"

I step off my bike, uncaring if I'm blocking the car pickup line and stand on the sidewalk. Pulling out my phone, I dial Lucy's number.

"Hey, sweetheart," I say when she answers.

"He won't leave with you, will he?" she asks with a chuckle.

"He's worried that something is wrong. I'm going to put him on."

I hand the phone to him.

"Momma? Micah is at my school... Yes, ma'am... I can? Really!... Yes, ma'am. I will... Hold on tight. I will. I promise... Yes, ma'am. I won't... Yes, ma'am... I love you, too. Bye."

He hands me the phone back.

"You've raised a good one, sweetheart."

"Take good care of him."

"Yes, ma'am," I tell her. "How are you feeling?"

"The bath helped," she whispers.

"Good. We'll be back soon."

We say our goodbyes, and I end the call.

"A few rules," I tell Harley before I let him climb on.

"Yes, sir," he says, his full focus on me despite the loud kids all around.

"You have to sit in front of me. I'll have to wear your backpack."

"It's Mickey Mouse." He holds the pack up. "That doesn't embarrass you?"

"Coolest mouse ever," I say, holding out my hand and adjusting the straps as far as they go so I can get it over my arms. "When you get on, I need your hands here, but you can't touch any of the controls."

"Got it. Anything else?"

I look at my bike. "Nope. I think that's it."

He doesn't weigh enough to worry about having him lean with me on turns.

I hold my hand out, and we execute the complicated handshake we mastered yesterday while we were watching movies at his house. He's giggling when I lift him up and place him on the seat before climbing on behind him. I drop his helmet on his head, fastening it under his chin, and crank the bike. It roars to life, and squealing, excited kids wave at us as we slowly roll out of the pickup line. Not once does Harley pick up his hands from where I told him to keep them to wave back. I don't know if he's following the rules I set forth, or if he's realizing that he doesn't need friends who will now only like him because he rode off on a motorcycle when they couldn't be bothered before.

I promised Lucy slow, and that's exactly what Harley gets, but you'd think we were racing down the turnpike at a hundred miles an hour with the way he's squealing. I usually go from one stop light to the next at a faster speed, but the child is six, and I'm not taking any chances with such precious cargo.

Knowing Lucy needs a little time to herself when she's not either sleeping or working, I take the scenic route to the fast-food joints in town, grabbing Harley and I a couple of burgers and fries before heading to the park. We eat at a picnic table, and I tell him he can go play, but he seems just as content to sit beside me and watch a couple of squirrels chase each other through the grass. He's a chill kid, and I wonder how much of that is because Lucy has to work nights and is tired during the day. I know they do outings on Saturdays, and he gets plenty of recess time at school. I know she's doing the best she can. God, I just want to give her more. She has to be utterly exhausted, never getting a real break. I doubt the woman has ever had a vacation in her life.

"None of them," Harley says when I ask him what his favorite subject in school is.

"Are you struggling?"

He gives me that *are you serious* look. "It's too easy. I'm bored all day, and when I draw, I get in trouble."

I keep my mouth closed. I could say a lot on that subject but saying it to a six-year-old isn't where the energy needs to be directed. Also, I don't know that Lucy would appreciate me getting involved. I'm sure she's said something to the school in the past.

"What do you like to draw?"

He shrugs. "Cartoon characters. Monsters. Dogs. Do you draw?"

I chuckle. "I'm no good at drawing. I'm good at working on bikes. I was a good soldier."

"I want to be a soldier."

"Not an artist?"

He shrugs.

"There's a kid at school and his dad is a soldier. He said his dad makes a lot of money."

Not working for the government, he doesn't.

"They have a really good benefit package," I say instead.

"I just want to take care of my mom."

"That's noble."

"What are your intentions with my mom?"

I choke on a sip of my soda. "My intentions?"

He nods, his face a mask of seriousness as he rolls a French fry between his fingers.

"I really like your mom."

"I don't want her to get hurt."

"I don't plan on hurting her."

"I know my mom and dad won't get back together."

I nod because I was wondering if he had thoughts about this, but I wasn't in any position to ask. His mother said as much but little kids have different viewpoints.

"Dad is coming home soon."

This makes me wonder what idea of *home* Harley has for Robbie Farrow once he's released from prison. This is another thing I don't feel like I have the right to ask. I haven't been in their lives long enough to ask.

"Do you think your mom likes me back?"

His grin is wide, giving me hope. Harley nods. "She gets this silly look in her eyes every time we talk about you. It's that same look the girls at school get when someone mentions Ryder Jones."

"Good to know," I tell him before taking another sip of soda.

"Do you think you can take me to get a Christmas gift for my mom? I've been doing chores for Mrs. Greene to earn money."

"Of course I can. Today?" I look down at my watch.

"I won't get all of my money until closer to Christmas."

"You tell me when, and I'll make it happen."

"Thanks." He looks out over the grass again, his little eyes searching for the squirrels that disappeared while we were having our serious conversation.

"We better head back before she sends out a search party for us."

We gather our trash and head back to the bike. I go back over the rules once again because safety is important before we head out of the park.

At a red light, I lean closer and ask Harley what kind of food his mom likes the most. He says barbecue, but she doesn't get it very often, so we end up at the best place I know of in town. He isn't very helpful when we walk inside, saying meat when I try to get specifics. We end up with so much, I can barely fit it in my saddlebags, but we somehow manage.

He's just as happy on the ride back to his house as he was the first time.

Lucy is waiting on the porch when we pull up, but Harley waits for me to lift him off the bike, so he doesn't burn his little legs on the exhaust. He scrambles to her, talking a mile a minute about his exciting ride and about his early dinner and even the squirrels at the park.

I gather the food from the saddlebags and carry them up the driveway.

"Dinner as promised," I tell her, holding up the bags.

"Are you feeding the neighborhood?" She raises her eyebrow.

"I figured you could take some for your lunches this week. It's not peanut butter and strawberry jelly but brisket sandwiches are good, too."

Her teeth dig into her lower lip. "I love brisket."

"There's smoked chicken and sausage in there as well. Harley didn't know what you liked best."

She looks over her shoulder, checking for Harley's location before turning back around to press her mouth to mine for a quick but sweet kiss. "You're amazing, you know that?"

I grin against her mouth. "You make it easy, sweetheart."

Chapter 9

Lucy

"You know the drill," the guard says as she hands over the two visitor passes. "One hug upon hello, one upon leaving. No contact in between."

I nod in understanding, handing over my limited personal belongings. We don't bring much with us when we come to visit Robbie. I don't want to risk anything getting stolen out of the car, and we aren't allowed to carry anything on our person but change for the snack machine during visitation. That change is in case Harley wants a snack, but he seldomly asks. Robbie has never asked, and the one time I did try to put money on his commissary, he refused it. He never wanted my help. He feels guilty enough for using the money he makes working inside for his own personal needs, but I completely understand. He has to survive. He swears he'll help when he gets out, but I'm more nervous about him staying clean and out of trouble. He struggles with that a lot. I've never been to prison but having a lot of freedom in an unstructured environment never worked for him before. It's going to be the true test for him.

"Daddy!" Harley yells when he sees Robbie, but our son knows not to run through the room.

We walk slowly toward the table we've kind of claimed as ours.

Harley throws his arms around Robbie and they squeeze each other for a short period of time, releasing the other before the guards get involved and tell them to split up. There are visits where Robbie has had harder months, and he holds on a little too long to his son, and it draws more attention. He must have had a good month because this isn't one of those times. He gives my shoulder a quick squeeze as we sit.

Smiles are easy all around the table.

"How have you been?" he asks me.

"Good," I tell him honestly because I'm the happiest I've ever been.

I'm nervous. I know Harley is going to mention Micah, and although I thought about asking him not to mention him, I knew it wouldn't be fair to ask a child to keep secrets from his father. I don't know how Robbie is going to react.

"How have you been?"

"Living the dream," he says, but there's no animosity in his tone.

After the first year or so, Robbie accepted his fate and has tried to see his sentence as a time to grow and get better, to get clean and work on himself in a way that when he's released, he's a better person. He's honestly found himself, and I think he was looking for that man when he turned to drugs all those years ago. It took getting sentenced to prison and getting sober to actually get there. It could've gone either way. I know there are days he struggles. He's mentioned in his letters to me more than once how easy it is to get drugs, how there are temptations everywhere he turns.

It gives me hope that he can be successful on the outside, that it won't be such a culture shock for him.

"How are you doing in school, Harley?"

Our son scowls, crossing his arms over his chest.

"That good, huh?" Robbie says with a laugh.

He looks to me, and I shake my head, letting him know that he still isn't making friends.

"I got to ride a motorcycle!"

I honestly thought I'd have a little more time than five minutes into our visit.

Robbie's eyes dart to mine. It's been almost a week since Micah picked him up from school, and he hasn't stopped talking about it. He's been a little disappointed each day when he saw my car outside the school instead of that bike. Micah sends laugh emojis each time I text him about it, offering to pick him up, but I don't want to burden the man.

"It was a very slow ride," I assure Robbie.

"Was this like a carnival thing?"

Robbie keeps his eyes locked on mine as he shifts his weight on the metal bench across the table from me. He's getting agitated.

"It was Micah's bike."

"Who's Micah?" His eyes are still on me.

"Momma's boyfriend."

"He owns a motorcycle?"

"Two of them. He's a biker."

My son is so helpful and just full of details.

"A biker?" Robbie asks, knowing what it could mean.

All of his trouble started with bikers in Santa Fe. Bikers are the reason I moved away from the area when I found out I was pregnant with Harley. It's why I choose to drive several hours to come visit instead of living closer.

"I don't want my son around bikers," he says, his voice as calm as he's able to manage.

I take a deep breath. I know where he's coming from. I know what he's thinking. I just need a minute to get my thoughts in order. Robbie and I don't argue. We never really have. Even when he was on the outside, we didn't argue. He was always too high. If I told him to get out and leave, that I was tired of his shit, he just left. He had other places to be, other women he could be with. He was too laid back to worry about me. There was no reason to argue. He was nonconfrontational. Fights weren't worth the wasted energy.

Robbie is no longer high. He's invested in his son as much as he possibly can be.

He lowers his head, inching closer. "You promised to protect him from that life."

"Harley," I say, looking Robbie right in the eye, no sour inflection in my tone as I reach for some of the change in my pocket. "Can you go see if the snack machine has any candy you like?"

"I'm not—"

"I'd really love something chocolate," I interrupt.

He takes the change from my hand.

The second he scoots away, I give Robbie my full attention. "Micah is nothing like the men you got tangled up with. They're good men. They help the community. They do fundraisers and buy playground equipment for local schools. He served eight years in the military."

"My cellmate served twelve years in the military, and it didn't stop him from killing his wife, Lucy. Who do you have around my son?"

"The Cerberus MC is well respected in the community, Robbie Farrow. You do not get to dictate who I date. I'd never put Harley in danger."

"M&Ms, Momma," Harley says as he returns.

"Those are my favorites. Thanks, sweetie," I tell him with a smile as he sits back down beside me.

Robbie clears his throat, and I know it's his attempt to get his emotions back under control. The visit continues, and he doesn't say another word about Micah or motorcycles.

"I've got a release date," he says when they announce the five-minute warning.

Harley squeals in delight, gaining a glare from one of the guards. He settles when I place my hand on his arm.

"Really?"

"First week in January."

"That's really soon." My heart rate skyrockets.

"Less than a month," Harley whispers. "I can't wait."

"I'll be coming to Farmington."

"I figured Las Cruces," I say. "That's where your family is."

"My family is in Farmington." His eyes challenge me. "I've served my entire sentence so I won't have to worry about parole, so I can go where I want."

"You can meet Micah!" Harley adds helpfully.

"Can't wait," Robbie says, his eyes on mine.

Chapter 10

Snake

"Hey," Lucy says when she opens the door.

She looks tired as she steps to the side.

"Where's the little man at?"

"In his room getting his shoes on."

I don't waste a second pulling her to my chest and pressing my lips to hers. In seconds, I'm hard in my jeans, the heat of her body warming me up. I'm glad I drove the truck today instead of the bike. It means I'm not wearing leather, making it easier to feel more of her.

We've spent at least two hours together every weekday morning this last week after she got off work and sent Harley to school. I was worried about her being tired, but she assured me she slept better after spending time with me. Wednesday, she fell asleep before I left, so I just stripped right back down and crawled in bed with her. Staying up late to text her on her breaks has been wearing me down as well, so we both slept until her alarm went off to go pick Harley up from school.

She wasn't upset at all that she woke in my arms, so we did it again Thursday and Friday.

Yesterday, however, was her day to drive to Santa Fe so Harley could visit with his dad. When I offered to take them, she turned me down immediately. Now she's pulling back from the kiss way too soon.

"What's wrong?"

"Just tired," she says as she steps out of my arms.

I trace the shadows under her eyes, pressing my lips to each of them.

"Are you going to tell me what you two are up to today?"

I shake my head, leaning in to whisper, "Christmas surprises."

She grins. I step closer to kiss her again, but the sound of Harley's excited feet pounding down the hall makes me take a step back.

"To be continued," I whisper.

She doesn't smile.

"Ready to go?" he asks, his face bright and unaware of the weird mood his mother is in.

"I'm ready. Grab your coat."

I squeeze her hand, wishing I knew what she was struggling with so I could fix it.

"Listen to Micah and behave," Lucy says as we leave.

The ride to the shopping center is filled with little boy chatter, and I participate as much as I can, but the topics change so quickly it's hard for me to keep up.

Prepared, Harley knows exactly what store he needs to go into.

"I saw her looking at this set," he says, tugging on my hand, pointing at a pair of earrings and a necklace.

Once we arrive at the jewelry case, he digs into his pocket and pulls out a small wad of crumpled bills.

"I have enough to get them both."

We spend a couple of minutes straightening the money before he hands it over proudly to the cashier, explaining that he had to sweep a lot of floors and wash a lot of windows for Mrs. Greene to earn this money.

Next, I take him to the gift-wrapping station in the corner of the strip mall and pay to have the items wrapped.

"You got her such great gifts, now I don't know what to get her," I complain as we window shop along the strip of stores. "Any ideas for me?"

Like he's thinking incredibly hard, Harley taps his little finger against his lips. "She likes sandals. The strap on her purse broke last week."

"Okay. Both great ideas. I don't know if we'll be able to find sandals in the middle of winter, but we can check."

We head to a department store, and I was wrong. Apparently, sandals are always for sale in New Mexico. I find her a pair of the slip-on kind, praying she wears a medium and a purse that the salesclerk assures me matches because what the hell do I know about fashion? We head back to the wrapping store and have those wrapped in coordinating paper to the first two gifts.

Hoping she just needed a little time to herself, I try to waste as much time as possible in the shopping area, paying attention to what makes Harley's eyes sparkle. Not once does the little guy ask for anything or even hint that he'd like a certain gift. He's such a gracious kid. I know he said thank you a dozen times when I bought him a burger and fries the time I picked him up from school, and you'd think I handed him the world when I made those small purchases at the tree lighting ceremony.

I want to spoil his ass for Christmas, but I don't want to show up Lucy. I want to spoil her too, but I don't want him to feel like his gifts weren't good enough. What a hard fucking place to be in right now. He worked so hard for that money, so it wouldn't be right to give him more and tell him to buy her something more expensive.

Shit. I don't know what the right thing to do would be.

"My dad is coming home."

I trip over an invisible line in the concrete.

"What?"

"My dad. He's getting out of prison."

"Soon?"

"First week of January. We went to visit him yesterday."

I knew this was why I didn't get invited over. I don't think she was hiding it from me, but it never came up in conversation either. We've had the month off from missions with Cerberus going into the holidays, and I've been completely focused on her. I just assumed that I'd spend the day with her. She never texted. I figured she needed some space since we spent every day this week together.

Did something change? Did they have a conversation about what that looks like, his getting released? Is that why she's different this afternoon?

After making the circuit of the shopping center, we return to the truck, stopping to grab dinner before heading back to her house. I promise to keep the gifts safe and hidden in my truck until Christmas, and Harley seems satisfied with them in my care.

Her mood is no better when we get back, but Harley doesn't seem to notice as he settles in front of the television to watch cartoons.

"Hey," I tell her, pressing my hand to her back as she stands at the kitchen sink. "Can I stay the night with you?"

Her head shakes immediately. "I don't think that's something Harley needs to see."

"What about staying after Harley goes to bed? I just want to talk." She shakes her head again, her throat working on a swallow. "I can tell you're upset, sweetheart. If we don't talk later, just talk to me now. Whatever it is, I just want to fix it."

"I'm just tired. I did a lot of driving yesterday. Everything's fine."

The kiss of death.

Fine means nothing is fine. I know women enough to know that much.

She turns to face me, pressing a soft, emotionless kiss to my lips. "We're going to have an early night. I'll see you soon."

Dismissed.

I brush my finger over her cheek, wondering if this is the end of what we got started, and by the time I make it through the little house to tell Harley goodnight, I feel like I weigh a thousand pounds.

The drive back to the clubhouse is brutal, every cell in my body urging me to turn back around and demand that she tell me what's going on. I hate not knowing the problem. I hate leaving her when she's hurting.

I don't even enter the clubhouse when I pull onto the property. I head straight for the garage, knowing that's where I'm going to find Skid and Ace. I know going to them for relationship advice is like going to a buffet for a salad. I'm going to end up with a lot of junk, but I'm not going to bother any of the other guys. Kincaid and Shadow have babies to worry about. Dominic has Jasmine and another baby on the way. Itchy is recovering from being shot, and I don't want to catch Snatch giving him mouth-to-dick resuscitation. Kid and Khloe never leave their room when they're home. You'd think they were teenagers who have to sneak around to get naked.

Ace and Skid will have to do.

"You look miserable," Skid says the second I walk inside the garage.

Maybe this was a terrible idea.

I flip the switch for the overhead heater. "Why do you have it so fucking cold in here?"

"Makes the blue balls more bearable," Ace answers. "Are your balls blue, too? Is that why you have such a sour look on your face?"

"She's being distant," I mutter.

"Move on," Skid says after handing me a beer. "There are always more women."

"Especially ones you don't have to sneak around and fuck," Ace adds.

"I don't have to sneak around and fuck her."

"You have to make a schedule. Can only go to her house between certain hours when her kid is at school."

I glare at my best friend. "Dating a woman with children is different from dating a woman that doesn't have kids."

"I fuck women with kids all the time," Skid counters.

"Women who parent their kids and women who leave their children to party and be raised by others aren't the same," I remind him.

"Are you sure you aren't clinging to this one because of what happened a few months ago?"

I continue to glare at Ace. "Why are you bringing Roxy up?"

"Isn't it obvious?"

"No. Why don't you explain it?" I take a long pull from my beer.

"Roxy gets pregnant, has an abortion, but she doesn't tell you about it until after the procedure is done."

"I still think that's fucked up," Skid mutters.

I look away from Ace, a spot on the wall becoming very interesting all of a sudden. "That decision was Roxy's alone to make."

"For your kid," Ace argues.

"Her body," I spit.

"I think you're projecting. I think you're going after Lucy hard because she has that ready-made family you want. She has what Roxy took from you."

"I didn't want a kid," I mutter.

"Until you lost a kid," Ace says.

Fuck. Roxy telling me she was pregnant lit me up. I was terrified, then excited, so excited, that I didn't comprehend her use of the word in the past tense. I ask her why she didn't tell me, and she said I was a playboy. She cried, regret spilling from her face in salty rivulets down her cheeks. She confessed that had she known I would've been happy, she never would've made that choice. I never felt like a bigger piece of shit. That's when I took a step back and took a long hard look at how I was living my life. I never had a problem with how I was "dating" until that moment. What kind of man was I if women saw me as the type that got a woman pregnant, and their first instinct was to abort because they never thought I'd be the type of man to step up and take accountability for a baby we made together? It was a solid kick to the nuts.

"I really like both of them. I'm not projecting. I want to see how this plays out, but she may not even give me the chance."

"Invite her to the Christmas party," Skid says.

"Not like we're going to have extra women there anyway," Ace says, bitterness lacing his tone.

"That's gonna suck," Skid adds. "Honestly, I joined this club because of all the easy pussy."

"There's easy pussy at *Jake's*," I remind him.

"The easy pussy was in the clubhouse, man. I don't like having to work for my meals. I'm a veteran for fuck's sake."

Ace and I chuckle. Skid is one of the hardest working men we have in the field, but he's lost as hell when it comes to sex. He's more of the point to his dick and raise an eyebrow kind of guy. Drive to *Jake's* and flirt? He'd rather stroke off in his bed and pass out with jizz on his chest.

I pull out my phone, shooting off a text to Lucy asking if she and Harley would like to come to the clubhouse for the annual Christmas party. I expect her to ghost me, but her acceptance comes only a few short minutes later.

Maybe things will get better. Maybe she was just tired and needed to get some sleep.

Maybe everything is *fine*.

Chapter 11

Lucy

I have no reason to be upset or frustrated. I told Micah I was tired, and when I did it earlier today, I wasn't lying. I'm completely drained. It's more of a soul deep depletion than a physical one though. I have no idea what I'm going to do once Robbie is released from prison. I was just starting to get a life of my own, and after six years of being single, raising Harley alone, I could picture sharing myself with someone else.

The banging on the door doesn't surprise me. I haven't known Micah for long, but he doesn't really seem like the type of man to let me stew in a bad mood. We spent days in each other's arms talking and getting to know each other. The man has had his mouth on nearly every inch of my body. The intimacy we've shared in such a short period of time has left me wanting more, but I can't help but pull back from him because I don't know what my life is going to look like once my ex is released. I don't want trouble for any of us.

I sigh as I pull open the door, but it isn't Micah standing on the porch.

"Robbie?"

Confusion draws my brows together as I look at the man I've only seen sitting across from me at a metal table in a maximum security prison for the last six years.

His throat works on a swallow, and he has the wherewithal to look ashamed.

"I know I shouldn't have showed up here unannounced."

You think?

I look over his shoulder, for a second wondering if the police are going to storm the house looking for him. It wouldn't be the first time.

"You're out?"

"They upped my release date. I didn't have time to get a letter out."

"And the phones at the prison weren't working?" I don't bother to hide the irritation in my tone. We just saw him yesterday. He had to have known he was getting released today. I can't help but wonder if this is the old Robbie standing before me.

"I wanted to surprise Harley."

"He's sleeping." I know Robbie has very limited experience being a father, but I won't wake the child up just because he shows up on the front stoop at nearly midnight.

"Lucy, can I come in? It's fucking freezing out here."

Robbie wraps his arms around himself tighter. The man is wearing non-descript jeans and a thin flannel, and I pause for a long moment before stepping aside and giving him access to the house. I'm not physically scared of him, but there is a hint of worry coursing through my veins of what this man can do to our lives. Hell, he's already causing problems with the way I sent Micah home earlier without explanation. I just couldn't bring myself to talk about Robbie getting released from prison and what it could mean.

Robbie doesn't go far into the house. If anything, he seems a little shy to be alone in the entryway with me. At least he isn't taking liberties in my home. I'm grateful for that. His eyes look around the room. From here, he can see nearly the entire place—the living room to the right and the kitchen to the left.

"Is Micah here? I'd like to meet him."

"He doesn't stay overnight, Robbie."

He nods as if he approves. By the time we left our visit yesterday, he seemed resolved that there wasn't much he could do about me dating again while he was locked away. Now that he's released, I have no idea what kind of trouble he may cause.

"You didn't know you'd be released today?"

He faces me fully. "I swear I would've told you. They came to my cell today and told me to pack my shit. I didn't question it. You don't argue about something like that. Harley is sleeping?" His eyes dart down the hallway, and I inch myself in that direction.

"He has school tomorrow," I remind him. "I don't want to upset his schedule."

"Yeah. Okay."

"Where are you staying, Robbie?" I ask it in a way to let him know that there isn't space available here.

We've had this discussion before, and at the time he agreed, but when those conversations took place, he had a plan. That plan didn't include an unscheduled release like he faced today. My eyes dart to the couch, and I already feel myself caving a little. I hate myself for the lack of resolve.

It's freezing outside, and he is the father of my child, but we're toxic together. There's not even an ounce of sexual tension or chemistry between the two of us, and after what I've experienced with Micah, I can't believe I ever even thought there was something akin to that with Robbie. I don't want him in my house. I don't know where I'm headed with Micah, or if I can salvage what's going on between us after the way I shoved him out of the house earlier, but I'm not going to burn what we have down by letting Robbie stay in my house.

"The counselor I was working with, you remember the one I told you about?"

"I do."

"He set me up with a guy here in town. He has a place for me to stay and a job waiting for me."

"That's good," I say as relief washes over me. I didn't want to have to argue with the man.

"It'll only last about a month, and then I'll have to find something else, but I'll manage. I always do."

Those words should make me feel relief, but they don't. *Always managing* for Robbie meant bad news in the past. It meant stealing, dealing or some form of criminal activity.

"I was just excited to see him for the first time outside of those walls, you know?"

"I know. Maybe tomorrow after school? He gets out at—"

"Daddy?"

We both look to the mouth of the hallway. Harley is standing there, rubbing his eyes, a look of surprise on his face.

"Hey, buddy," Robbie says. "Did we wake you?"

"Why are you here?"

Robbie chuckles, but it seems pained. I don't doubt he's a little hurt that Harley didn't just race across the room and run into his arms, but his being here is completely out of the norm for the child and anything outside of his routine is suspicious to him. It's why he wouldn't get on the motorcycle with Micah without speaking to me first. The kid is naturally suspicious.

"They released me early. Aren't you happy to see me?" Robbie squats down, putting himself more on Harley's level instead of walking closer, and I appreciate him giving Harley the opportunity to come to him rather than forcing his proximity on our son.

"You're done in that place?"

"Finished."

Harley's eyes look up to mine, and tears start to form. "Can I stay up just a little while?"

I nod. "Just a few minutes."

Harley runs into Robbie's arms, his eyes squeezed tight as he hugs his father.

I know Robbie probably wants a little time alone with Harley, but I've been present for every single minute they've spent together. I'm not willing to step away from that level of supervision just yet, but I don't sit right on top of them as they chat. I busy myself in the kitchen, putting away the dishes I washed after dinner.

Harley talks a mile a minute, showing his dad the movies we've purchased recently from garage sales and the card games he's collected over the years. Robbie is the one to pull the plug on the visit after a half an hour, and I don't know if it's because he's trying to keep to the short time schedule I set or if it's because he's already growing weary of being here. He stands, gives Harley one more hug before sending him back down the hall to his room with a promise of seeing him again soon.

He turns toward me, a serious look in his eye once Harley is out of the room.

"I still want to meet this Micah guy."

I nod, in no mood to argue this late at night or list Micah's positive attributes. I did that yesterday during the prison visit. If there was something wrong with the man I'm dating, Robbie might have a leg to stand on or a position to tell me not to have him around Harley, but that's not the case. Micah is nothing like how Robbie used to be. He's a good man. I don't feel the need to justify him.

"School releases at three fifteen. I leave for work at ten fifteen, but Harley goes to bed at eight thirty. I wake him to go to Mrs. Greene's right before I leave for work."

"I can stay with him while you're at work."

"He goes to Mrs. Greene's. That's his routine. That's how it's going to stay."

He nods in agreement. "Okay."

"Do you have a phone? I think we need to communicate when you're coming over."

"Don't want me just randomly coming over?" He gives me a weak smile, and I know he's just teasing me.

"I have my own life, Robbie. You're going to have yours as well. There will be boundaries."

"I know. I'll see about getting a prepaid tomorrow. Sleep well, Lucy. See you tomorrow."

I press my forehead to the door after he leaves, but no matter how many slow breaths I take, the weight on my chest doesn't lift.

Chapter 12

Snake

Lucy: I just need a little time and space.

I've read that text message over and over for a week and a half.

We went from can't get enough of each other to a complete stall in our relationship, and I easily call it a relationship because I can't get the woman out of my head. Never in my life has a woman had me so damn tangled up. I mope around the clubhouse like a kicked dog. Ace and Skid make fun of me. The other guys avoid me because my attitude is awful. I'm a walking advertisement for the premedicated people on anti-depressant commercials.

I hate feeling this way. I hate that I've driven by her house on numerous occasions. I hate that I know Robbie Farrow is out of prison and is spending time at her house. I hate that I asked Shadow to do some research on the man. I hate that she won't talk to me and tell me what's going on herself.

More importantly, I hate that things may be over between us when we barely got started in the first place. I pictured myself starting a life with this woman. I know it was early days, but white picket fences and a yard full of kids? Yeah, I wanted that with her. I wanted the sink full of dishes and toys spread out around the family room. I wanted the dog getting into trouble for chewing the corner off the couch and baby giggles. I wanted soccer games, and hell, trying to get along with her ex because it was clear from watching Robbie play with Harley in the front yard that the man loves his son.

I want all of it.

I'm tired of slinking around in the shadows not knowing where I stand. She needed a little time and space, and I gave it. A week and a half is a little, at least by my standards, and enough is enough.

I thought about walking away, that maybe fighting for what I've imagined isn't worth it, but those thoughts make me sick to my stomach. I know what we have is special. I can feel it every time I look at her. Giving up on her isn't an option. If that's what she wants then I'll have to deal, but I need to hear it from her lips.

I watch as she walks Harley next door to Mrs. Greene's house, my restraint barely under control as she climbs into her car. I keep some distance between her car and my truck, thankful that she's a very punctual person, arriving fifteen minutes early to work each day. It will give us a few minutes to talk without me causing her to be late to work. I just want to know where we stand without making her late. I don't want to cause undue stress. I want to make things easier for her. I want her to know that I care, that I'm here for her.

I know she's too stuck in her head when I manage to get within a few feet of her as she climbs out of her car without her noticing me.

"Lucy?"

She gasps, turning in my direction, relief washing over her when she notices it's me. The company she works for seriously needs to replace the burned-out lights in the employee parking lot.

"Hey," I say stupidly as if we're running into each other on chance and I haven't been stalking her up to the exact moment she arrives at work. "Can we talk?"

Her eyes dart around the parking lot.

"I'm not going to hurt you."

Her face falls. "I... Micah, I wasn't even thinking that."

"Robbie is out of prison." I'm not going to waste time because she doesn't have much before her shift starts.

"He wasn't supposed to get out until January, and he just showed up the Sunday after our visit. He wants to meet you, but it's complicated."

"Complicated how? Are you two getting back together?"

She shakes her head, an instant reaction. "No, but he was around bikers before, and that's how he got into trouble."

"I'm not going to be best friends with your ex, sweetheart, and we're not criminals. He's not going to be in trouble with us. If he's got a record, he can't even come on Cerberus property."

She shakes her head. "That's not what I mean. He just has all these preconceived notions, and I don't know. It's just. Ugh." Her hands go to her face.

"I'll do whatever I need to do to prove that I'm not a bad influence on Harley," I tell her, hating the two feet of distance between us.

Just a few weeks ago, we were naked in her bed. There wasn't even a whisper of space between us and now the distance seems like a mile.

"You don't have to prove anything."

"I have to do something, sweetheart. I hate not seeing the two of you. I hate this time and space."

She sighs, and that's another thing I despise right now—her frustration with this whole situation. I came into her life wanting to make things easier, not cause her more stress.

"It's what I need right now."

"Baby."

I step close.

She inches further back.

I drop my hands, somehow knowing that she's not going to give in. I can't push her further away. She's already teetering on the edge of breaking this off completely.

I won't let her go. Doing so is impossible, but I can give her what she needs in the moment.

"I'm here when you're ready, Lucy."

It's difficult to walk away and not kiss her, not assure her with my lips on her skin that she has all of me.

I can't even look back at her when I climb in my truck because then I wouldn't be able to leave. I'd end up on my knees begging, and it wouldn't end well. She's a stubborn woman. She's done too much on her own to need me the way I've grown to need her. I feel her strength, and I hate that it's the one thing that's keeping me at arm's length right now. I don't want her weaker. I'd never wish that for her but being needed wouldn't be so bad either.

I'm bitter by the time I get back to the clubhouse.

The garage is empty when I sit down with a beer, but before long others start to filter in. Oddly, Itchy is one of them. He's well on his way to recovery now after being shot and nearly dying. I'm happy to see him closer to his normal self, but it's weird to watch Snatch walk in and kiss him right on the mouth.

"That's one way to get around the 'No Women in the Garage' rule," I mutter.

Snatch kicks my boot before sitting in the chair between Itchy and me.

"What's your damn problem, anyway?"

"His girlfriend told him she needed space," Ace pipes up.

I snarl in his direction. My best friend has no damn business spreading information about me.

"Her old man just got out of prison," I explain.

Shadow narrows his eyes as he leans forward in his chair. "Something we need to worry about?"

"I don't think so. They got divorced shortly after he got sent up for dealing drugs. Been inside for a decade, but she said he wasn't the nicest fucker before he was locked up," I explain. That's not the full story, but it's close enough. Lucy said he was in and out for the last ten years. She got pregnant in between those times, that's how Harley is only six, but the finer details don't really matter.

"From what I can see," Ace cuts in, "she doesn't have anything to worry about. She took their boy to visit the whole time he was in, and she says their relationship is amicable, but she was a little nervous about him getting out and seeing a biker hanging out at the house all the time."

It looks like I talk too much when I've been drinking, something I've done too much of since she declared her need for time and space. Ace, no matter how drunk he is, remembers every damn thing.

"Let us know if he becomes a problem," Kincaid says.

"I will," I grumble. "I just hate being away from her."

It's the truth, and with most of the guys here in serious relationships, I don't feel like a pussy for saying that out loud.

"How old is her son?" Dom asks.

"Ten, I think," Ace answers for me, getting it all wrong. The man doesn't know shit about kids. Harley doesn't even look close to ten. Hell, he's small for six. I don't correct him. "Goes to Dolchester Elementary."

"That's where Jasmine goes," Dom says. "I wonder if they know each other."

"Couldn't tell you that," I say. "There are so many kids around I can't keep up with shit."

"More to come," Shadow says, grinning around the mouth of his beer. "Three more months and my little boy will be here. A week or so after that, Dom's son will be here."

"Like I said, so many kids." I toss my empty beer bottle into the trash and grab another.

"You don't need to be involved in her life if you can't handle her kid," Dom chastises.

"I just miss them. Haven't seen her all week, and phone sex really isn't my thing," I lie, making it out like we've had more communication than we've had. I don't want to look like a complete wuss in front of them.

Itchy chuckles. "So we get to the root of the problem."

"Could always hook up with the blonde from *Jake's*," Ace offers.

"No thanks," I mutter. Do other women even exist any longer?

"What about you guys?" I ask Itchy and Snatch, trying to get the attention off of me. "You ever plan on having kids? I mean adopting or some shit."

"No, man. No kids for us. Don't get us wrong, we love playing uncle to all the wonderful kids around us, but we aren't the daddy type."

As if on cue, the baby monitor sitting beside Kincaid activates, and the small whimper of one of the girls can be heard through it.

"Nice chatting with you guys," Kincaid says as he stands. "But my sweet angel is awake."

"She doesn't sound very happy," Snatch says when the whimpers turn into full-on wails.

"The joys of parenthood. Ivy is teething, and it's as if Gigi feels her pain because she's fussy and upset too," Kincaid explains. "See you assholes in the morning."

We all say our goodnights as he leaves the garage to go take care of his girls.

"You guys looking forward to that stage?" Snatch directs his question to Dom and Shadow.

They both grin.

"I can't wait," Dom says just as Shadow says, "Not a chance."

Shadow looks over at Dominic. "You have no idea what you're asking for."

"I spent twenty years in the Marine Corps. I can handle an infant."

Shadow just shakes his head in disbelief. "Okay, then. When you realize how hard and exhausting it is, I won't even be an asshole and tell you I told you so."

"You staying over?" Ace asks Dom as he stands and grabs another beer from the fridge.

"Yeah. Jasmine said Ollie was missing Matilda, so we're here so they can visit." He smiles, knowing he's wrapped around that little girl's finger, and not giving one single fuck about it.

"You're going to end up with a litter of damn dogs at that house of yours, if you're not careful," Snatch warns.

He chuckles. "Yeah, I think we're past that. That dog's stomach is already swelling. But what can I say? Matilda and Ollie love each other. I can't keep them separated. Griff loves Ollie so I can't bring him home with us. Besides, Em would never let him leave the clubhouse overnight. So, because my damn dog is head over heels for the dog here, I'm stuck with you assholes tonight."

"Not stuck with me," Shadow says as he stands from his chair. "Misty is waiting on a foot massage."

"Yeah, I'm sure Mak is ready for me to rub her back," Dom says, getting up from his chair as well.

"Sweetheart," Itchy says in a sarcastic tone as he stands, holding his hand out for Snatch. "Ready for me to massage your cock?"

"Jesus," Dom mutters with a laugh.

"What?" Itchy asks with a wry smile. "His feet and back are fine."

Snatch swats his hand away playfully and stands up. "Only if you do that thing with your tongue."

I groan because a cock massage sounds pretty damn good right now.

All the married and taken men disappear, leaving just Ace, Skid, and me in the garage. Silence surrounds us for a long time as we drink beer. I'm thinking about Lucy and how much I miss her. Ace's mind is probably blank because the man has the uncanny ability to think about literally nothing. Skid is no doubt wondering if it's worth it to get up and go inside to sleep or if he can just pass out in the chair he's sitting in.

She agreed to attending the Christmas party, but with the way things are going, I doubt she's going to follow through with that. As the seconds tick away, I can feel her slipping away.

Chapter 13

Lucy

I hate breaking promises, but I must've known when I told Micah I'd go to the Christmas party that I wasn't going to attend because I never told Harley about it. I always do my best not to disappoint my son. I hate seeing his face fall and watching him try to hide his displeasure. Never mentioning it meant I knew deep down I didn't plan to go.

I feel more than a little guilty about that.

Micah: Okay.

That was the only response I got when I texted him, telling him that I wanted to keep to the Christmas Eve traditions Harley and I have always had. There have been too many changes this year already, and I didn't want him to have too many more.

I expected him to try to persuade me to still come. I sort of wanted him to, but he didn't. Is this him doing what I asked, giving me time and space, or is he giving up? Is that what I want? I'm so conflicted and torn, I don't even know.

I'm worried for Harley, but he seems to be taking everything in stride. He asks about Micah constantly, bringing him up in front of Robbie like it's no big deal to mention mom's boyfriend to his father. It stresses me out, making me wonder if I'm the one with the problem and not our child. Robbie has asked on several occasions to meet him, but I keep putting him off. I told him the last time he asked that we're taking a break. I don't know why I'm not seeing Micah. My reasoning felt solid at first, but now nothing makes sense.

Maybe I just don't want my two worlds to collide. I don't want Micah to see what I used to be. He's heard the words. He knows I used drugs in the past. He knows Robbie and I got married while we were high because it seemed like a great idea. He knows that Robbie was in and out of my life as much as he was in and out of jail. I made a lot of bad decisions. Robbie made even more.

But somehow, turning that from just conversation into something visual, something tangible, makes it real. It could ruin us.

Pushing him away could ruin you, too. If you're not careful, you could lose the best thing that's ever happened to you.

I shake my head, trying to get rid of that thought and smile at Harley as he opens the worn cardboard box we stored the Christmas tree in last year.

"Need any help?" Robbie asks.

Harley shakes his head. I grin at his independence. The tree we have isn't very big, but he's a little guy.

I'm trying not to be bitter about Robbie being here and inserting himself into our traditions. I knew it was going to be like this, but I got so used to it just being the two of us. I feel a little uneasy with the changes.

Robbie smiles as Harley struggles to push the box over to make it easier to remove the tree.

"If you make a mess—"

"I clean it. I know, Momma."

I laugh.

The Santa Clause plays on the television—another tradition we started two years ago—as Harley finally gets the tree out of the box. Robbie helps with the stand because that part is impossible for Harley to do on his own as I start unwrapping the ornaments we have.

One by one, I hand them to Harley as he decides where they need to go. I feel bitterness settle in my stomach when Robbie lifts our son to place the star on top. I'm not supposed to experience this on Christmas Eve. The holiday is about love and cherishing who you're with, but this isn't what I pictured going in to tonight. I want Micah here beside me, his hand in mine as Harley plugs in the lights for the first time on the little tree.

Instead, I have my amazing son staring at the tree and Robbie looking a little agitated because despite his best intentions, he struggles with being a dad for more than an hour at a time. He's honestly just not used to being around kids. He's responsible for his own structure and choices, and after years and years of being told what to do and when to do it, he doesn't know what to do with his freedom. He confessed that he's fine at work. He has tasks and within those confines he does well. It's the hours after the work bell rings that he struggles.

"Now it's time for hot chocolate," I say as I get off the sofa.

"What about gifts?" Robbie asks, his eyes searching mine.

He knows how hard we've had it all these years.

"I forgot mine back at the house, but I'll bring them over first thing in the morning."

I nod. There goes another tradition I have to make accommodations for.

"Santa comes at night, but I have to hide mine from Harley." I playfully glare at my son who has the decency to look guilty.

"Really?" Robbie asks, facing Harley.

"It was only once. I was curious. In my defense, I was four."

"Sneaky," Robbie says, ruffling his hair.

"Robbie, do you want hot chocolate?"

"I need to get back to the house," he answers.

"We have to do reindeer food first!" Harley disappears down the hallway, rushing back with his backpack.

"Reindeer food?"

"They make it at school," I explain.

"It's oatmeal for the reindeer and glitter so they can see our house from the sky. I don't want Santa to miss us!"

"You have to put shoes and your jacket on," I remind him as he rushes for the front door.

Robbie helps Harley into his jacket after he slips his shoes on without socks. Robbie tugs his jacket on last after handing mine to me.

"Thank you," I tell him, giving him a weak smile.

I wonder if he can sense my unhappiness. I know Micah was able to the second he saw me the day he took Harley on the super-secret trip the Sunday after our last visit to the prison, but Robbie hasn't said a word to me about it. Maybe he doesn't read me the way Micah does. Maybe he doesn't care that I've been feeling a little lost and broken. I mean, we aren't together, so maybe it's not his place to be worried.

"Let's go," I say to Harley as he waits patiently by the door.

"Look," Harley says with awe when the front door is opened.

To the right of the door is a stack of gifts, and the second I spot the motorcycle ornament sitting on the very top, I know who they're from. I look up and down the street, but I don't see his bike or the truck he drives. I hate that I missed him. These weren't here when Robbie arrived, and he's only been here for an hour and a half. I feel empty knowing he was so close so recently, and I didn't get to see him.

Harley and I should be with him tonight, but I texted that I wanted to stay home. I regret that now more than ever.

"These two are from me, Momma." Harley points to two perfectly wrapped gifts sitting on the top.

"I love them."

"You don't even know what they are." He giggles. "These two are from Micah."

He points to a couple more in similar paper. So, this is what they did on their little outing. What a sweet man to include my son on something like this.

"I don't know what these others are."

Robbie bends down, reading the tags on the other gifts. "Those are all for you, kiddo."

He's smiling as he says it, but I can see the strain around his eyes. I can imagine what he's feeling. He's not getting rich working for the man the counselor set him up with when he was released, and he's not getting a free ride either. A lot of his paychecks are eaten up with bills and rent. He had to buy clothes with his first check, and it didn't leave much left over.

"He's not trying to show you up," I whisper to Robbie. "He's a good man."

Robbie nods, his eyes darting away from me to watch Harley as he scouts out the front yard, looking up at the sky for the best angle to place the food.

"He seems like a good man from what you've said and from the way Harley talks about him. I wasn't able to get him much, Lucy."

"He never expects much. He's a grateful kid."

He shakes his head, and I know he's disappointed in himself, more now that he's on the outside and struggling. It makes me wonder if he's going to start pulling back, distancing himself from Harley because he doesn't feel like he can do right by his son. I wonder if Robbie feels like anyone can do better than he can.

"Robbie." I reach for him, but he steps off the porch.

"How about this reindeer food? Do we put it in a pile or is it more of a sprinkle?"

"We sprinkle it," Harley explains to his dad. "But wash your hands before you rub your eyes. Glitter hurts really bad if it gets in your eyes."

"Noted," Robbie says as Harley sprinkles some in his hands.

They spend thirty seconds spreading the "food" out for Santa's crew before Robbie waves goodbye. He's been walking back and forth from where he's been staying. I don't offer to drive him because money is tight for me as well and gas is expensive. He promised before he was released that he wouldn't be a burden on me, and he's been good about sticking to that. Financially, anyway. Emotionally, I feel like things couldn't get worse because I'm heartbroken. Robbie was here tonight instead of Micah.

I usher Harley back inside, urging him to wash the glitter from his tiny hands before getting ready to go to bed as I get the gifts from the front porch and situate them around the tree. We finish watching *The Santa Clause* and enjoy the hot chocolate.

"Will Micah be here in the morning when I wake up?"

"I don't think so, buddy."

He nods, his little face sad.

After getting Harley to bed, I pick up the phone and type out a text, thanking Micah for the gifts, letting him know that I'll get pictures of Harley opening them in the morning.

I get back a thumbs up.

It guts me.

I manage to get the hidden gifts out of the top of my closet, arrange them under the tree, and back to my room before I break down into sobs.

Chapter 14

Snake

Hangovers are the worst, especially after a night that's meant for happiness and fun. Fours kids were at the clubhouse last night. Shadow's son Griffin, Kincaid's twin daughters and Dominic's adopted daughter Jasmine. It should've been five. Harley should've been here with Lucy.

There was joy last night, even when Dom announced that the first sonogram they had last month was wrong and he wasn't having a son but a daughter. They're going to name her Sophia and are ecstatic that she's healthy.

Lucy didn't show. I knew she wouldn't. She texted earlier in the day saying she wanted some normalcy. I wasn't a part of that, but it didn't stop Robbie from being a part of their routine. The man they spent an hour with once a month for the last six years got to infiltrate that special night. I wasn't invited.

The day has been absolute shit, spent popping over-the-counter pain medicine and drinking bottled water to make up for the whiskey I drank last night like it would solve all of my problems. Even Ace and Skid left me to it after the party died down early. Everyone called it an early night because Christmas morning was fast approaching. Kid and Khloe disappeared because they couldn't keep their hands off each other. Snatch and Itchy had better things to do than watch me wallow in my heartache.

Jack Daniels was a shitty substitute for company and he did me wrong this morning. His companionship left me miserable and dehydrated. It'll be awhile before I meet up with that betraying bastard again.

The clubhouse is quiet, and I'm only half paying attention to the football game on the television. I'm watching the recording of it because I slept during the live version earlier. Lucy promised pictures last night of Harley opening his presents, but the images of him seeing his leather boots and various other riding gear never came. It's for the best I guess because he'll probably never get to use them, not with me at least.

If he was happy to receive them, I bet Robbie got to experience those smiles and that joy. I hate the man for it, but he's the kid's father. I wanted my dad around, remember longing for him on Christmas morning, hating the fake smiles my mom suffered through after his death. I don't begrudge the man for getting to be there with his son.

"We're heading to the bar," Ace says as he walks into the room, Skid close on his heels. "Wanna come?"

I roll my head on the back of the sofa. "No thanks."

I know exactly where I want to be, and it's not in a bar filled with lonely women.

I know she has to work tonight because there were still a few call centers open today despite it being Christmas day, and it wouldn't even be an option if she didn't have a shift. Harley is home, and I don't get to stay with her at night.

"Snake?" Ace asks from the front door.

"I'm staying here," I snap. "Get off my dick about it."

"You heard him, darlin'. He's not interested."

"I'm just—"

I pop up off the couch at her voice.

"Lucy?"

She gives me a weak smile, her cheeks rosy from the cold.

Ace winks at me as he steps around her on the front porch.

"Catch ya later!" My best friend gives me a quick wave, and he and Skid take off.

Tears are falling down her cheeks before I can get her inside.

"Did he hurt you? Where's Harley? I'll fucking kill him, Lucy."

She shakes her head, her eyes darting all around as if she expects someone else to be in the room.

"Come on," I tell her, my hand on her elbow as I usher her through the living room toward the hall. "We can talk in my room."

She comes easily, bypassing Snatch and Itchy who are in the kitchen getting something to eat without a word. Within seconds, we're closed inside my room. I flip the light on, my eyes raking over her person, checking for bruises or any sign that the motherfucker put his hands on her.

"I called in sick to work. Harley is with Mrs. Greene." Her eyes take in my room. "I expected the clubhouse to be more active."

"It was a couple of months ago." My head is a riot of questions and emotions, but if she and Harley are safe, we can get to why she's here at her own speed.

I swallow as her eyes search mine. If she's here to break things off for good, maybe it's best to just rip the bandage off and get it over with. I'm not one to shy away from pain, but I find myself scared to have my heart ripped from my chest right now.

She looks heartbroken as she drops to the edge of my bed, her focus now on her fingers as they tangle together.

"I didn't know I could feel the way I do, and then Robbie showed up."

"And you care for him."

Pain greater than I've ever felt before threatens to knock me right off my feet.

"There's no form of emotional connection to Robbie. I want him to succeed because he's Harley's dad, but when the high wore off, there was nothing left between us. I never lied to you about that. It ended years ago. We never should've gotten married."

I stay quiet because I'm confused. I don't want to speculate on where this is going.

"He's not going to stay in Farmington because there's no work for him here. After this job is done, he's going to have to move on." She draws in a shuddering breath, still refusing to look up at me. "He's a felon, and I'm not going to support him. Robbie would never ask me to do that, but I won't keep Harley from him either. He loves his dad."

I inch closer, knowing touching her right now probably isn't what she wants but I'm not able to stay away.

"I like what we started, but at the same time, it isn't fair to either of us."

"We don't have to make any decisions right now," I promise her. "Look at me, sweetheart."

She doesn't. Her head shakes, as if she's telling me it's just too painful to look at me.

I reach for her, lifting her chin with the crook of one finger.

"I don't give a damn about fair. I've wanted you since I first saw you at that damn gas station. You're gorgeous and strong, and you deserve this. *We* deserve this, Lucy. We deserve happiness."

She nods, and if it weren't for the tears on her cheeks, I'd almost be convinced that she truly believes what I'm saying.

"Can I hold you?"

She nods again, the only time she doesn't hesitate in her decision. She kicks off her shoes, and I do the same with my boots, and that's how we spend the next hour, her in my arms, her silent sobs shaking against my chest.

At some point, she turns in my arms, her breaths warm on my neck, her fingers tangled in my shirt, and when her lips meet my throat, I know she needs more.

I plan to give her exactly what she needs without making her ask.

Stripping her bare while lying down isn't the easiest thing, but I manage, first pulling off her jacket and shirt before moving to her jeans. I lick at her skin, tasting her, savoring her because I'm not a fool. I know there's a good chance this is goodbye. I heard her words. I listened even though I didn't want to understand what she was trying to say.

Her back arches when my teeth graze her nipple, her fingers working my own shirt up my torso. I take a break only long enough to pull it over my head and toss it to the floor, and then my mouth is on her once again.

"Get my cock out, sweetheart."

Her fingers immediately get to work, first on the button of my jeans and then my zipper.

"Missed you," she whispers, and it makes me want to growl in anger.

She didn't have to miss me. I've been here the entire time. This woman has me wrapped around her finger. All she'd have to do is text or call. Hell, send up a smoke signal, and I would've been on her doorstep in minutes. There was no need for either of us to have missed the other. We could be like this all the time. She's punishing us for no reason. Her guilt is misplaced. So, Robbie has to move for work. Big damn deal. Let the man work. It has no bearing on what we have.

"Missed you, too," I say instead, because telling her all that other stuff right now wouldn't go over well. "Need you, Lucy. Need you so bad."

And I don't just mean that I need to sink my cock deep inside of her. I need her with me, need her heart beating against mine. I need her smiles and her tears if that's the emotion she's struggling with. I need her to confide in me, to rely on me. I need *her*.

She tries her best to shove my jeans down, but her arms just aren't long enough. I have to leave her for a second to kick my jeans off and grab a rubber from the bedside table.

"Panties and bra off, sweetheart."

She disposes of them quickly as I roll the latex down my length. I plan to slide right inside of her, but shit, the sight of her center is honestly too good to bypass. I slide back on the bed, my intentions clear as I lick my lips.

She opens for me, legs spread wide, her fingers already reaching for my face, and I fucking love how her hands cup my jaw when I taste her like this.

I groan with the first lick, but then I get so lost in devouring her that sounds are no longer possible. She rolls her hips against me, the rhythm of the two of us the perfect choreography, something we mastered early on in her bed.

"Micah," she moans. "That. Do that again. Oh God."

Her body locks up, knees clamping around my ears, and I double my efforts until her core pulses against my mouth. I don't stop until it feels like she's going to rip my beard from my face. Her lazy smile and unfocused eyes are proof of a job well done when I look up at her. I don't waste a second slipping between her trim thighs.

My mouth covers hers as I slide home, my jaw tight with the sensation of her warmth swallowing me.

"Jesus, baby. Every time, it just gets better."

My hips move slowly. I'm going to savor every damn second I can get. I lick into her mouth, swallowing her whimpers and moans as she lifts her legs higher on my hips. Her nails scrape down my arms, and I don't care if she takes the ink of my tattoos with them. I love the bite of pain.

"Feel me, Lucy. Goddamn, feel me."

"Yes," she pants.

I want to demand that she tells me that she's mine. In this moment, I know that she will. She'd tell me whatever I want to hear. It's why I hold on to the words I really want to say because there's a chance she'd say them back. It would destroy me if this were goodbye. I don't want those words from her if they aren't a part of our forever.

For a split second, I wish I wasn't wearing a condom. I know she's not on birth control. That's another conversation we've had in the past. She didn't have a need for it because she wasn't sexually active. I want to fill her with my cum and pray that she's nothing like Roxy. I want her belly round with my baby. I want her tied to me like she's tied to Robbie, only I wouldn't end up in prison. The woman under me would have my ring on her finger. She'd be in my bed every night. The dream I had of babies and the dog chewing on the furniture would come true because I'd never let her go, but that's fucked up.

Trapping her into a life she may not want with me is next-level psycho.

It was just a flash, but the thought was there. I grind into her harder, deeper. I want her to feel me tomorrow. I want her to answer the door when Robbie knocks to visit his son and still be sore from where I've been.

"Micah," she moans. "Make me come."

Wrapping my arms around her back, I give her everything I have. In my mind, I say everything I can't utter out loud. In my head, she's mine. She clenches around me, her body fluttering down the length of me, and I try to hold off. I slow down, cherishing the way she feels as she orgasms, but it's just too good. She's just too perfect to resist following her over the edge.

I kiss her through my release, tasting her breathlessness on my lips as she comes down from her high.

Chapter 15

Lucy

I let myself get lost in him for a few minutes longer when I wake up in his arms. The strength and the warmth of them are almost enough to make me forget just how messed up everything else is, but reality won't stay in the darkness. Eventually, the sun will rise, and I'll have to face the real world.

He shifts slightly when I slide away, his face scrunching in displeasure when I manage to free my body from under his arm. Finding my clothes is easier than I anticipate because he tossed them all in the same direction. Other than our clothes, there's nothing else on the floor. His room is remarkably clean for a single man.

I can't look back at him as I pull my jeans on. I already don't want to leave. Seeing him one last time would be unbearable torture. Once fully dressed, I reach for the doorknob.

"If you're going to leave me, at least face me when you do it." His voice doesn't hold the hint of sleep like I expect it to. He's probably been awake since I climbed out of the bed.

The tears I thought I got control of last night are already falling by the time I turn around.

"Why are you crying? Don't cry if they're lies."

"They're not lies," I assure him, wiping angrily at them.

"Then don't make this goodbye."

"It has to be."

He shakes his head. "It doesn't."

"I want more."

"I'll give you the fucking world, Lucy. You have to know that."

"How is that fair? How can we keep doing this when I'm going to have to leave?"

"Leave? You don't have to leave."

"Robbie will have to leave."

"Then fucking let him."

He's not raising his voice, but I can tell that it's taking a lot not to.

"He's Harley's father."

"I'm not arguing that, but you're talking about what's fair. How is it fair for you to chase after him? To uproot your son? That's not fair to him."

Slapping me in the face would hurt less.

"It's not fair that you have to be unhappy just because Robbie Farrow made bad life choices."

"None of this is fair, but Harley needs his dad."

"And I need you. Fuck, Lucy. Don't you see that? And I need Harley, too."

"We barely know each other."

He nods, his face suddenly becoming an emotionless mask. "If that's what you truly think, then maybe you should go."

I watch him for a long moment, hesitant to walk out of here, but I really do need to leave. Had I gone to work, my shift would've ended fifteen minutes ago. I should already be at Mrs. Greene's house picking up Harley.

My son is and always will be my number one priority. Maybe one of these days, Micah Cobreski will understand that's why I have to walk away from him today. What I want, and what I need doesn't matter. My happiness comes second to Harley's. Even if my heart is breaking. If his heart is smiling, then it's worth it.

"Goodbye," I whisper as I turn to leave.

It's early enough that I make it out of the building without running into another soul.

I cry the whole way home, and there's no way to hide the destruction on my face when I pull into my driveway. I take a few minutes to myself, dabbing fast-food napkins from the glove box under my eyes, but they do nothing for the redness and swelling. I always try to hide my pain from Harley, but it'll be impossible today.

I have to clear my throat four times before I open my car door to make the tears stop, but at least my face isn't wet when I knock on Mrs. Greene's door.

"Momma?" Harley asks the second he opens the door. "What's wrong?"

I smile down at him. "Would you believe me if I said nothing?"

I clear my throat again, hating that I'm going to lie to him but telling him the truth isn't going to work either.

He shakes his head.

"It's really not a big deal, but they got a new cleaner at the office."

He sighs, a long deep exhale of air. "Let me guess, it has a lemon scent, and you forgot to wear one of those masks."

I shoot a finger gun at him and smile, hating that I've used this excuse so many times over the years with him. Being a single mother is hard, and sometimes the bad days outweigh the good.

He shakes his head. "One of these days, you're going to learn."

"One of these days," I echo.

I give Mrs. Greene a wave, nodding when she mouths, asking if I'm okay, and we head across the yard to our house.

"Do you need a nap?"

I shake my head. Despite the emotional rollercoaster I've already been on today, I slept very well in Micah's arms last night. I need to stay busy today to keep from calling him and telling him everything I said was a big mistake.

"Let me get a quick shower, and we can go grab breakfast, maybe go to the park or something."

I wash as quickly as I can, refusing to look at myself in the mirror. I can still feel him on my skin, and I don't doubt with the way he spent extra attention with his mouth on me that that was his intention all along. I dress in something warm, thinking I can use up some extra energy walking laps around the playground equipment while Harley plays, before heading back out to the living room.

I stop right at the end of the hallway, finding Robbie in the living room. I've always told Harley not to open the door, but I never told him not to let his own father in the house.

"No work today?" I ask casually.

"Job's done."

I frown. "Already? I thought you said it would last a month. It's barely been three weeks."

He shrugs. "Got it done quicker. Gotta look for something else now."

"We're getting ready to go for breakfast and then the park. Wanna come?"

Robbie's eyes roll up to me, but I turn before they can meet mine. I won't make the decision for him, but I hadn't planned on there being three of us today.

"Sounds like a fun time. We can kick the new soccer ball I got you for Christmas around the park," Robbie offers.

I've discovered that Robbie is a fan of doing things with Harley that don't require speaking. Harley asks a lot of questions, and Robbie doesn't always know how to answer them. Apparently, even keeping your nose clean in prison still comes with a lot of dishonest and sneaky behavior. He recognizes it as such and doesn't want Harley knowing those things so he's out of the loop on how to give sound fatherly advice.

"Is it in your room? Go get it," Robbie urges.

I head to the kitchen for a glass of water and something for the headache that started forming the second the tears began falling before I left Micah.

"Hey," Robbie says, following me into the kitchen. "Did you work last night?"

I turn to face him. Noticing his eyes on my neck, I know what he sees. I got a flash of the mark there on my way out of the bathroom.

"I want to meet him."

"It's over between us," I assure him.

"I don't have to go with you guys today."

"It's fine."

"My treat," he offers. "I insist."

I nod. I won't argue about the man paying for breakfast, and I don't see it as a favor. I've taken care of Harley his entire life without a penny from him. We're due little something from the man. I refuse to feel guilty about that.

Harley joins us in the kitchen.

"I think I want pancakes."

"And bacon," Robbie adds. "Maybe sausage."

They talk about food all the way to the diner. I've found it's an easy subject for them, one that doesn't trip either of them up. I'm able to hide the tremble in my hands as I climb out of the car, but my eyes dart toward the two bikes parked on the far end of the lot.

"Maybe Micah is here!" Harley says excitedly. "You can meet him, Daddy. We haven't seen him in a long time."

Our son rushes for the front door of the diner, his eyes darting all around when Robbie holds the door open for the two of us.

I don't know if I'm relieved or saddened when I don't see any guys in familiar leather cuts with a three-headed dog on the back. The waitress seats us quickly in a corner booth, and Harley is a little more animated than he normally is. This is the very first time we've gone out to eat as a family. We haven't been back here since those two guys were jerks to me, and Micah stepped in.

I'm looking at the menu, wondering if I should be petty and order something expensive when the sound of male laughter makes my head draw up. The missing leather vests are drawing closer to me. The two guys that were with Micah that day are exiting the bathroom, both smiling and laughing at something one of them must've said before they walked out. They have to walk right past our table, and I realize they know exactly who I am when the laughter stops the second they notice me.

I don't dart my eyes away even though I want to. I left Micah in his bed less than two hours ago, and I already long to go back to him. I want to scoop Harley up and leave Robbie at this table. I want to tell him to figure his shit out, but I can't do that. Doing so would be selfish.

They both nod at me and keep walking.

"Those are Micah's friends," Harley supplies helpfully. "Momma, go ask them where he's at. Maybe he can join us for breakfast."

My eyes meet Robbie's for a quick second before I drop them to the menu again.

"Pancakes or waffles?" Robbie asks as if it will be enough to distract him.

It won't be.

"Momma? I need to tell him thank you for the gifts. I'm wearing my new boots."

"I'll text him after breakfast," I assure my son.

"Scrambled or fried?" Robbie continues, and I want to strangle him.

"Scrambled," Harley answers. "I don't like my food trying to run away from me."

I jump at the roar of the motorcycle engines despite them being outside, and I can't concentrate on the menu in my hands until they drive off and I can no longer hear them. Breakfast is a sad occurrence. I order oatmeal and juice because there's no point in wasting anyone's money when I can't taste it. Robbie doesn't try to carry on a conversation, and Harley seems content to color on the paper kid's menu.

The park is pretty active since so many kids are out playing with new Christmas toys. Harley, being the sweetheart he's always been, is just as excited for his new soccer ball as the other kids are with their new expensive drones and remote-controlled cars. Robbie is awful at soccer, and before long, Harley finds another kid willing to play with him and gives his dad a break.

"If I had half his energy," Robbie says as he falls to the bench beside me.

"Seriously," I mutter, keeping my eyes on Harley as he plays.

I had every intention of walking around the park, but I'm just not feeling it now.

"I'm sorry for you having to do this all by yourself all these years." I can feel his eyes on me, but I refuse to turn my eyes to him. "You've done really well with him."

I nod. It's the best he's going to get.

"I know he wouldn't be as well rounded as he is if I weren't locked up."

Now I turn myself to face him.

"That's where you're wrong." He frowns. "I will always put him first. Even if you were out and pulling all the stupid shit you pulled back then, he would've come first. He would be exactly who he is now despite who you ended up being."

He nods, swallowing as he looks away. "He's lucky he has you."

"I've made a lot of sacrifices for that child, and I'll continue to do so, but I swear, Robbie, if you start this poor me bullshit right now, I'll lose it."

"The fuck am I supposed to do, Luce?"

"Be better. Do better. Get a job. Be there for your son."

"That shit's hard."

"Life is fucking hard, Rob. Welcome to reality. I didn't quit. I never gave up. I'm not going to sit here and give you permission to. He won't understand if you do. He won't forgive you if you do."

He turns his face back in my direction. "Okay."

Simple.

I think it's the realest conversation we've ever had.

Chapter 16

Snake

Sleep after she left was impossible, but I didn't chance climbing out of bed. Sitting up meant putting clothes on. Getting dressed would only lead to me grabbing the keys to the truck. I wouldn't jump on my bike because it would be impossible to scoop both her and Harley up and drag them back here until she listened to reason. The truck would be the only way to accomplish that.

So, I just lay in bed, for hours, my eyes glued to the ceiling while I ran through scenario after scenario of how to make this work out in our favor. Ours, not just mine. She was hurting when she left, and not because she was hurting me. She wanted to stay. She wanted to be a part of what we were building, but she was afraid of what she would be taking away from Harley if she did. I'm a selfish fuck.

My first instinct was to tell her that he only saw Robbie's ass once a damn month for an hour. I could make that happen. I could keep that same damn routine up for the kid no matter where Robbie landed. He could live in China, and I could do better than that. I didn't understand the damn problem.

But Harley has been spending more time with his dad over the last couple of weeks. That schedule had already changed. Harley deserved every person in his life that loved him, even the man who messed up so badly that he couldn't be a functioning part of his life for the first six years.

I just want to be a part of his life as well, and fuck, I love the woman.

I love her. I'm *in* love with her.

I know that's crazy.

I know if I told her that last night, she wouldn't have stopped with her hand on the door like she did. She would've hauled ass out of here so fast, she would've set the carpet on fire.

It's too soon, too fast, but damn, if it isn't love that's eating its way through my chest, then what the hell is it?

I know I've never felt it before. I know I'd live the rest of my life in misery if it meant the woman never cried another tear. I'd lay down my life right now, no questions asked, if I could guarantee her happiness, if she never suffered ever again, if Harley was provided for the way he deserved.

And then it hits me. I know what I have to do. It'll kill me, but as they say, sometimes love hurts.

***

I've said a lot of things to Kincaid and the other men I work with in Cerberus over the years. Many things I regret, things I never should've let slip past my lips. A lot of those things I never thought twice about until someone else called me out on it.

Today, my hands won't stop trembling as I wait for them to enter the conference room. When they do, I think about bolting, calling the entire meeting off. I'm second-guessing myself, and as a man who has always trusted his gut, this goes against my nature.

Kincaid steps in first, clapping me on the back as he walks past.

"Did you have a good Christmas?"

"The bonus was nice. Thanks for that," I tell him.

"Of course. You guys work hard. You earned it." He sits in his usual spot at the head of the table, waiting for the others. "Did you hear about Dominic? A little girl. Can't believe they messed that up. Two daughters aren't the end of the world though."

I give him a weak smile. I know the man is just making casual conversation, but it's the last thing I can manage with what I'm facing right now.

Shadow is next to answer. He looks utterly exhausted, but that doesn't keep a smile from his face.

"Hey, man. Good Christmas?"

"Can't complain," I tell him.

Another lie. I can complain for days, but I'm a man of action. I'm not here to drag them down into my pity party. Shit needs to be done, and I need to make that happen.

Dominic is next. Not one for many words, he nods at me as he passes. Kid closes the door when he steps inside the room.

"Snatch and Itchy?" I ask.

"Itchy has a follow up doctor's appointment," Kincaid explains. "We can postpone until this afternoon if you need them here."

"No. It's fine," I tell them, waiting for Kid to take a seat.

Kincaid leans forward in his seat. "This seems serious. Are you quitting? I don't want to lose you. We have plans in the works to get more men on the team."

"I'm not here about me."

Kincaid frowns, and I know that he doesn't miss the fact that I haven't answered his question.

Shadow drops down in his seat in the corner of the room, and I give him time to fire up his computer. He's going to need it for the favor I'm going to ask.

"The other night we talked about Lucy Farrow." Kincaid nods, and I do my best to ignore the sound of Shadow's fingers working over his keyboard. "Robbie Farrow was recently released from prison. He's having trouble finding work in town."

"Not much around here, especially not for an ex-con," Kincaid confirms as he looks over his shoulder at Shadow.

"Robert Farrow, twenty-nine. Just released from the Santa Fe super-max after serving just over six years for drug charges."

"Super-max for drugs?" Dominic interrupts.

"Had some seriously violent behaviors in jail and prior offenses," Shadow explains.

It proves my initial reactions to her showing up crying last night as being on point, even though she was here to tell me goodbye not because he hurt her.

"He had some trouble once he got there, but then he seemed to have gotten his shit together. Worked as a machinist at the prison. No write-ups in five years. Monthly visits from Lucy and Harley Farrow," Shadow continues.

"That's their son," I add.

"Former drug addict," Shadow says as he lifts his eyes to mine. "Is he clean now?"

I shrug. "I don't know. I'd like to say yes. I don't think Lucy would let him around Harley if he were using. She seems to think he's a different guy than he was before he went down the last time."

"What do you need from us?" Kincaid asks.

"He needs work. Can you find him something?"

"He can't work for Cerberus, Snake. He's not even allowed on the property, changed man or not," Dominic says.

"I know," I say, looking up at him. "I know. From what I gather, he'll do anything."

"It won't be in Farmington," Kincaid adds. "Is she going to follow him?"

I nod. "She will."

"Out of state?"

I nod again. "Yeah, man. She's not going to keep Harley away from his dad. He doesn't fucking deserve her, man. She's one of the good ones."

"Sounds like it," Shadow says as his fingers continue to work.

"You're sure this is what you want?" Kincaid asks.

"I need him to be able to take care of his family. She's struggled long enough. I don't want him bouncing from place to place, and them trailing along after him. They need stability." My throat feels like it's going to close up on me.

Kincaid nods, as Dominic steps closer.

I stand before he can reach me.

I swear to God if he clamps a hand on my shoulder, I'll lose my shit. I'm barely holding it together right now as it is.

"I'll see what I can find for them," Shadow says. "I'll let you know."

"You're a good man, Micah Cobreski," Kincaid says.

I give them a quick nod before I leave the room and disappear down the hall. I have nothing in my stomach, but that doesn't keep me from bending over the toilet and heaving the second I get back to my room.

I think I just made the biggest mistake of my life.

Chapter 17

Lucy

My coffee has gone cold, but I'm still holding the cup in my hands, pretending that I'm drinking it. I'm hiding from my son because being in the same room with him means that he may ask questions. I hate myself for it. Normally, I'd be right there with him, giggling when one of the animated characters on the movie he's watching does or says something silly. I'm losing time with him because I can't get things right in my head.

The three days since I walked out of the Cerberus clubhouse have been miserable. I've spent them wondering if I've done the right thing, spent them telling myself that texting or calling him to come over is the worst idea in the world. If it weren't still Christmas break, I know I would've caved by now. My body aches to be close to him. My heart breaks a little more knowing he's right across town, and I'm the one putting the distance between the two of us.

He said he wanted both of us, not just me. He included Harley in that as well. He's nothing like any of the men I've met before.

"You're sad."

I look up at Harley, hating the frown on his young face as I lift my cup of coffee to my lips.

The cold liquid is bitter on my tongue, but I do my best to hide my distaste.

"We need to talk," I tell him, deciding right in this moment that I can no longer keep everything from him.

He can't be a part of the adult decisions I have to make, but I can at least keep him informed.

"Is this about Micah?" he asks as he pulls out the other chair at the small dining table.

"Some of it."

"He hasn't been around much."

"I'm not seeing Micah anymore."

"Did you guys have a fight?"

"We didn't, but some things are going to change, and it just isn't going to work out between us."

"I liked him." Harley hangs his head, pouting only the way a six-year-old can.

I hate seeing him sad, and it makes me regret bringing a man into his life only to have Micah leave so quickly. I wasn't thinking this would be the outcome. I make a mental note to do better next time, but the thought of there even being a next time makes my stomach turn.

"We're going to have to move."

This news gets no reaction out of him.

"Does that not concern you?"

He shrugs, his tiny shoulders hitching as if it doesn't even matter.

"The kids at school are mean to me. They probably won't even notice I'm gone."

As if my heart couldn't break any further.

"I guess Micah won't be coming with us?"

"No, Harley. Micah lives here. Your dad has to find work."

He finally looks up at us.

"And we have to go where he goes?" His little brows draw in, confused. "Why? Can't we just go visit him like we used to?"

I realize now who the child would choose if he had to pick between Micah and his own father. Micah plays soccer with him without getting tired after fifteen minutes. He holds conversations with him without having to look to me for help. He has two motorcycles. He took him shopping for Christmas gifts.

It's not that Robbie is a bad guy, but he's not very good at the dad thing. Robbie is almost scared to be a dad, and he gets flustered very easily. Harley loves his dad, but I think he's more comfortable and accustomed to spending time with him in a controlled setting.

"You don't want to move?"

"Can Micah come with us?"

I sigh, having already answered this question.

"No, Harley. He can't."

Harley nods as if he's trying to understand. He's trying to be strong because he doesn't like to upset me, but he's young and frustrated. He rarely asks for things, and I wonder if he's been building up all those asks for this moment right now, for the one thing that's impossible to give him.

I know following Robbie to wherever he finds work is selfless. It's helping my ex and giving Harley time with his dad, but I can't help but wonder if it's the wrong choice for all involved. Was the pep talk I gave Robbie the other day at the park the wrong way to go? I know it would hurt Harley if Robbie walked away, but would it be better in the long run? What if Robbie really messes up down the line? Is it better for him to give up and walk away now?

I've second-guessed a lot since Harley was born, and this is just another one of those things. Only this time, my gut is torn on what's the right decision because I can't tell if my choices are muddled because the decisions now involve things I want and things I feel Harley needs.

I wasn't going to ask Harley what he wants because it's unfair to put the weight of that on a child so young, but he's making it clear what his position is. As far as he's concerned, he can have the best of both worlds. He can stay and have Micah in his life, and he can keep with his routine of seeing his dad once a month. Nothing has to change.

I drop my head into my hands, the throbbing that has been a constant for nearly two weeks at the base of my skull threatening to get worse.

"I'm going to go watch TV," Harley mutters.

I can't even lift my head to acknowledge him, and that's another way I'm being unfair to him. He deserves better.

I'm zoned out, wishing for a miracle when a knock echoes through the small house. I no longer get excited that Micah may be on my front porch, and when I stand from the kitchen table, I notice that Harley doesn't even pull his eyes from the television.

We both know it's Robbie. He's the only one that's been coming over. I pull open the front door and step to the side, but he doesn't give me the soft smile he normally greets me with.

His face is animated this afternoon, and I immediately step in front of him. I recognize that look. It's one he's had numerous times when he was high as a kite.

"No," I tell him, blocking his entry into my house.

Emotions clog my throat. He hasn't even been out of prison for a month, and he's already back to his old ways. I should be livid, but a rush of relief washes over me. If he's going back to his old ways, then so can we. He can disappear, and we don't have to move.

"I'm not," he whisper-hisses, reading my mind, but his actions are jerky, his hands shaking as he bounces on the balls of his feet. "I have great news."

"Robbie," I warn. "I'm not doing this with you again."

I'm facing him fully, so Harley doesn't see what's going on, pleading with my eyes for this man to not ruin what innocence I can preserve for our son.

"I haven't been using, Luce. I swear. I got a call. I just got a really good job."

I take a long look at him, searching his eyes. His pupils are normal size. His skin is his normal color, cheeks a little pink from the cold. His lips are dry and cracked.

"I'm just really excited. I didn't think I could find work so quickly, and I didn't think I'd find something so good. The benefits are great. Medical, dental. Even a really good retirement plan. Lucy, it's going to be great. I'll be able to take care of you guys."

"I don't need you to take care of me."

"I can take care of Harley. Pay back child support. Whatever. It's going to be awesome."

"What kind of job?"

Deciding he isn't stoned, just thrilled to share his good news, I step aside because it's freezing outside.

If he found something so quickly, then it must be around here, and that gets me excited as well. I smile because things like this don't happen for me. Things don't work out for me. I'm always forced to make a sacrifice.

"Offshore oil rig," he states as he steps inside, raising his hands to his mouth and blowing on them to warm them up.

"Like in the ocean?"

He nods, his smile wide, eyes bright and beaming.

"We live in New Mexico."

"The job is in Texas. Well, offshore in Texas."

"Texas?"

He nods as if he's won the lottery, and he's still trying to wrap his head around it as well.

"What?" That screeched word comes from Harley, and we both turn to see our son standing to the side with tears rolling down his cheeks. "I don't want to move to Texas."

"It'll be fun, buddy. You can swim in the ocean."

Harley shakes his head violently before running up to Robbie. He pulls back his little leg and kicks Robbie right in the shin. Harley's eyes widen dramatically before he spins around and runs to his bedroom. His door slams, but the walls are so thin, we can both hear his little sobs.

I stare down the hallway in shock because Harley has never done anything even remotely violent in his life before. I don't know how to react. Do I punish him?

"I thought he'd be excited," Robbie mutters as he bends forward and rubs the spot on his shin. If he's not going to make a big deal about it, then neither am I.

"Change is hard for kids," I say because I refuse to lie and say that he'll get over it. I also won't tell him about the conversation I had with Harley earlier. "When do you start work?"

"In a week."

"A week?"

Robbie is still smiling. "I'll go ahead of you guys and make sure everything is lined up. I was told they provide room and board for families."

"We are not living together, Robbie."

"I'll be offshore nearly all the time, Lucy."

"Absolutely not."

His smile widens. "I figured you'd say that. It's a duplex. Any problem with living next door?"

I huff. "You're an asshole."

He chuckles, but then his face falls when he looks down the hallway. "Is he going to be alright?"

"I hope so. I'll have a chat with him."

Robbie leaves only a few minutes later because sticking around for a serious conversation with Harley would be just too much of a parent thing to do. I'm not winning any parenting awards either because it takes me twenty minutes before I go into his room to speak with him. He refuses to talk to me, so I just sit on the edge of his bed and rub his little back until he falls asleep.

Chapter 18

Snake

I'm a patient man. Three weeks ago, nothing bothered me. I was happy-go-lucky. I lived life in the moment. I went with the flow. Now? Every damn thing gets on my nerves.

I don't realize how bad I've gotten until I consider tilting over the fridge when the automatic ice machine in the freezer drops ice into the tray and then refills, the sound more annoying than ever today.

"You seem tense," Kincaid says as he enters the kitchen, heading for the coffee pot.

And not once since joining Cerberus have I wanted to punch my boss in the nose for just speaking.

He cocks an eyebrow at me as if he can read my mind when I turn to face him. I see the challenge on his face, but I only consider it for a second.

"I have news, but it doesn't look like you're in the mood for it." The slow stir of his spoon through his coffee makes me want to flip the fucking table.

"Will waiting change anything?"

He shakes his head.

"Might as well get it over with then," I mutter.

"We were able to lock down a job for Robbie Farrow."

I nod, knowing they'd be able to find something for him.

"It's in Texas, offshore oil rig."

I grind my teeth so hard I wonder how much more they can take before they crack.

"Shadow was able to find a duplex for them to live in, so they can live really close to each other." He watches my face as he takes another sip of coffee. "He'll be out on the rig a lot, but he'll be right next door and can see the kid easily when he's home. He'll be right there if Lucy needs anything."

My knuckles turn white as I grip the table. I manage a nod, but I'm not sure if it's because I'm acknowledging the information he's giving me or the decision I'm trying to maintain not to kill someone.

Robbie is going to live right next door. Whatever Lucy needs, he'll be able to give her.

I could burn this fucking world down right now. She doesn't fucking need him. She needs me. Fuck, I know I need her. Goddamn it. This is the worst fucking place to be in the world right now. I feel completely fucking impotent, and I'm the one that set this shit in motion.

"Shadow was also able to work out a transfer for Lucy. Galveston has a sister company of the one she works for here. The one there actually has promotional opportunities. I bet she'll be a supervisor in no time. The school system seems good. I'm sure they'll do well in Texas."

Kincaid takes another sip of his coffee, his eyes never leaving mine.

I can't get past the feeling that every word from his mouth is a fucking challenge, but at the end of the day, I respect the man too much to throat punch him. I stand from the table, walking slowly to the sink to wash my coffee cup.

"Anything else?" I ask.

"I think that's about it."

"Thanks, Prez," I tell him before walking slowly out of the kitchen.

My body is a fucking live wire by the time I make it back to my room, but I manage to close myself inside and count to thirty. Slow breaths in, slow breaths out. Eyes closed, my future flashing nothing but black images of sadness behind the lids.

When I open my eyes, I'm nothing but a ball of rage. I destroy the room, ripping the bed apart. The television, the dresser, the curtains, nothing is a match for the pain and anger I feel.

Robbie Farrow makes every damn wrong decision, ends up in prison off and on for the better part of ten years and he still gets the damn girl. He gets the family that I want, the family I can take care of. I've always known life wasn't fair, but fuck, a break every once in a while would be nice.

I'm sweaty and heaving by the time there isn't a single thing in the room left untouched.

I'm not surprised by the knock on the bedroom door, only surprised it didn't come sooner, but hell, whoever it is could've been knocking for the last five minutes and I wouldn't have heard them.

"Yeah," I huff, my breaths rushing past my lips.

The door opens, and I slowly turn to see Ace with his head through the open crack. He doesn't seem surprised by the mess I've made. He must've been standing in the hall waiting for it to end before interrupting me.

"What's up?" I ask, raking my hand over the top of my head.

"This probably isn't the best time to tell you that Robbie Farrow is in the parking lot asking for you."

My laughter is menacing, and I know he can see it in my eyes as well.

"I'll tell him to leave."

"No," I say, stopping him before he can turn away. "Just give me a few minutes. I'll be fine."

He takes another long look at the room. "It's going to take more than a couple of minutes."

"Have him wait."

He nods at me before backing away and closing the door.

Fifteen minutes later and several rounds of breathing exercises a military therapist taught me after my first combat kill later, I feel just sane enough to walk out of my room. I count my steps down the hall and through the living room, taking another deep breath before turning the doorknob on the front door. Skid and Ace are nearby. I can't see them, but I can sense them, and I know that's for Robbie's protection, not mine.

I appreciate them for it because I'm still feeling a little unhinged right now. I've made more than my fair share of bad decisions in life, but nothing that would land me in prison. Today could be the day though.

The sight of Robbie Farrow doesn't surprise me. I've seen pictures of him, but it's clear he's never seen me. I want to give him the same dangerous smile I gave Ace earlier as I approach him, but it's not even needed I realize when his throat works on a swallow.

"Micah?" Robbie asks as I step closer. "Robert Farrow."

I look down at his hand, but I don't reach for it. The man isn't exactly stealing my girl, but at the end of the day, she's still leaving because of him. I'm not exactly feeling very welcoming right now. He's lucky I don't grab him by the back of his scrawny fucking neck and drag him into the street. I'm already going to catch shit for destroying Cerberus property, and him being here is going to get me in even more trouble because he's a felon. The rules are clear.

"You need to be a man."

I growl at the motherfucker. "You have a lot of fucking nerve."

He holds his hands up, and he must not be as fucking stupid as I thought if he can predict how close I am to kicking his teeth in.

"You need to go to her and beg her to stay."

"Sounds like you're the fucking coward if you can't tell her you don't want her to go."

I can barely manage the words without yelling them, but calm is my go-to before losing my shit.

"She wouldn't listen to me if I did that."

Robbie bends at the waist, and I'm seconds from snapping his neck when he reaches for his pant leg, but he doesn't grab a weapon. He lifts the denim to show me a tiny bruise on his shin.

"Harley kicked me yesterday when he found out I got a job in Texas."

I don't bother to hide my grin. If I ever get the chance to see that kid again, I'll give him a high-five for the act of violence.

Robbie drops his pant leg, straightening to face me once again. His face is sad, but I don't have it in me to feel sorry for the sack of shit standing in front of me. He made his choices and living with the consequences are just part of the cards he's been dealt. As far as I'm concerned, he's getting off a little too damn easy.

"I want to get to know my son better, Micah, but I don't want to do it at the expense of him hating me in the end."

My jaw ticks, but I don't say a word to him.

"I know you had something to do with getting me that job. The guy I work with mentioned your club, so tell me. Did you do it to get rid of me, or were you trying to get rid of her?"

My knuckles crack when I squeeze my fists. "I love that woman, and I love your son. I don't want her to suffer because you can't get your fucking life together."

He nods as if he expected me to say those words.

"If you love them, you'll fight to keep them here."

"I love them enough to let them go." I watch his face, and I can see the disappointment already forming in his eyes.

But he's not disappointed in me. He's already disappointed in himself. He knows he's going to eventually let them down. He's already given up on himself. I don't know if it's because he's already starting back down that black hole Lucy was so sure he'd crawled all the way out of or what, but he's come to the realization that there's no escape for him. Sooner or later, he's going to end up exactly where he started, and he doesn't want either of them to bear witness to his inevitable downfall.

"She'll end up hating me if I come between you and Harley," I explain, even though he doesn't deserve that from me.

I'll give him the credit that's due. It takes a lot of balls to show up here and ask this of me, but it still makes him a coward for not sitting her down and explaining all of this to her.

He's less of a man than I gave him credit for. I didn't want the man to fail. Harley deserves the best everyone can give him, but it doesn't look like that's in the cards for him.

"She'll hate me if I come between the two of you," he counters.

I won't kick the man while he's down, but I could see that hatred for him already forming in her eyes when she walked away from me last week. That seed was planted long before she showed up on the clubhouse front steps with tears in her eyes. When he made her feel guilty for wanting a little something for herself, when she felt selfish for wanting a little slice of happiness, she started to despise him.

"I guess no one is going to win in this situation," he mutters before turning and walking away.

Robbie climbs into an old beat-up truck that I know belongs to the man he's been working for and leaves the property.

"Everyone fucking loses," I mutter before heading back inside to face the music on the condition I left my bedroom.

Chapter 19

Lucy

"It's like a picnic!" I tell Harley as he frowns at me for the millionth time.

I've gotten nothing but frowns for the last several days. I haven't seen a smile since Robbie came over and dropped the bomb about going to Texas. He watches television with a blank expression. Even the parts that would normally make his sweet little giggles bounce off the walls have been absent. He didn't get excited when I told him he'd get to ride on an airplane for the first time, or when I showed him pictures of the house we were going to be living in that Robbie forwarded.

I shouldn't have researched online about his behaviors because now I'm worried my young son is depressed.

"It's a cardboard box," he mutters as he carries his plate to the living room.

"But we now have twenty dollars we didn't have." I wave the two tens in my hand, hoping he'll be excited by the cash.

"But we no longer have a kitchen table or chairs."

I frown when he turns his back to me.

"The house in Texas is fully furnished. Do you want to see the kitchen table we'll have there? We'll have six chairs."

"No," he says, not in a disrespectful tone, but he really just doesn't care.

As each day passes, he's less interactive. He answers when I speak to him, but you'd think each day he wakes up that his vocabulary is cut in half.

"A lady is coming by this afternoon to pick up the couch," I tell him, so he doesn't throw a fit when the knock comes.

He shrugs.

We leave for Texas the day after tomorrow, and of course I have my last shift at work tonight. I didn't want to give up any shifts, and I didn't want our routine to change any more than it had to. Harley will stay with Mrs. Greene one last time, and although I could see it in her eyes when I told her our plans, she hasn't opened her mouth to tell me it's a bad idea.

"When you're done eating, I need you to finish packing."

"I don't have much left. You already shipped more than half of my things." I never knew a child could sound so bitter.

"They should be waiting for us when we get there," I remind him.

I've done as much as I can in the short time period Robbie gave us in the last week, shipping what I could. It's been easier only having to send personal things and clothes since the house is furnished, but the stress level is still through the roof. Things are easy to relocate. It's leaving people that kills me.

We won't know anyone but Robbie. I won't have a Mrs. Greene to rely on if I need help. I can't even think about Micah without my eyes burning.

"I'm going to pack a few things in my room," I tell Harley, leaving my own lunch plate on the counter.

Once I'm in my room, I close the door softly. Being strong for him is one of the hardest things I've ever done. Each time he gets upset, or I catch him with tears in his eyes, I want to draw him to my chest and cry with him. I want to tell him things will be okay, but I can't guarantee that they will.

Leaving feels so wrong. It feels like the biggest mistake I could ever make. Wrong for me. Wrong for him. Hell, it feels wrong for Robbie, too. As the days have passed, I've gotten the distinct feeling that Robbie doesn't want us to go to Texas. He hasn't said as much, but his initial speech about taking care of Harley and medical and dental and retirement started to shift, taking on more of a *this is a lot of responsibility* tone than *one of being ready to face the world* he started with.

Harley hasn't mentioned Micah again, but I didn't miss the way his ears perked up when he heard a motorcycle ride by yesterday or the way his eyes got wet when it drove by without stopping.

I press my forehead to the back of my closed door, taking long deep breaths, willing myself not to cry because I know if I start, I won't be able to stop. I've had to be strong for Harley for so long it's become second nature, but I'm starting to wonder if I've used all of that up and the supplies aren't replenishable.

I shouldn't text him. I know I shouldn't, but I just can't resist. We're leaving tomorrow. That train is set in motion, and nothing will stop it, but I can't leave town without seeing him one last time. I just want to touch his face, to press my lips to his one last time. I just want him to hold me in his arms, to feel what it's like to have been loved one more time.

I fire off the text I may end up regretting, asking if I can swing by the clubhouse before my shift. He doesn't respond, and I don't even know why I was expecting him to. I walked away from him. I told him there was no chance for us. I knew if Robbie were going to leave town, Harley and I would have to leave too. With my son so angry with me, it seems like a stupid choice now, but things have to get better because they really can't get much worse.

I stare down at my phone for long minutes, knowing he isn't going to text back, and that's all the answer I need. He was always so quick to respond when I texted before. Even when it got closer to the end, after I told him I needed time and space and he only sent emojis and a simple okay, he was pretty quick. His non-answer is my answer.

I drop my phone on my bed and go back out into the living room. If I give myself the chance to obsess over it, that's exactly what I'll do.

Harley's chuckle stops me in my tracks in the middle of the hallway. It makes a little sunshine come back into my life, but then he notices me, and his face goes blank again. He's punishing me. I'll take whatever he can dish out so long as he's not really living in his own little personal hell twenty-four seven.

I head to the kitchen, pretending that I didn't observe his quick change in attitude and wash his plate from lunch, then I spend ten minutes actually tasting my own food for the first time in days.

I manage to stay busy in the kitchen for several hours, packing dishes to take to Goodwill before heading back to the bedroom to check my phone. When I pick it up, I gasp, shocked to have a text waiting for me from Micah.

He doesn't shoot me down or tell me to go to hell, but the hotel name and room number is just as weird.

I don't message him back a million questions although they're running through my head the entire time I'm getting ready for work.

Harley doesn't inch away from me when I sit down on the sofa beside him. I'm counting it as a win. I miss his smiles and his quick hugs. I miss the way he crawls in my lap and invades my space. I miss the millions of questions he asks and the way he's always asking me trivia questions. I just miss him.

I know we'll get back to that eventually, but I'm sad that we aren't experiencing any of that right now while we have the chance.

"I read online that your new school has three slides on the playground."

"I don't want to talk about my new school," he mutters.

"Okay. Well, go get your pajamas on. I have to head to work."

I'm not going to mention that I'm going to see Micah before work. It would only break his heart, and he wouldn't understand why he can't come.

It only takes a few minutes before Harley is back out in the living room with his pillow and favorite blanket. My heart is in my throat when I kiss him on the forehead as he settles on Mrs. Greene's couch for the last time. I'm near a panic attack driving across town. My heart is racing when I lift my hand to knock on the hotel room door.

Chapter 20

Snake

I'll never get over that feeling I get the very first time I see her each time.

The most beautiful woman I've ever set my eyes on. I love it when she looks at me. I don't care if she's happy or sad, angry or scared. When her eyes are on me for a split second, everything in my world is absolutely perfect.

Tonight is no different.

Even with the nervousness tightening her shoulders, there's a blink of time where our worlds aren't crumbling around us.

"Lucy," I whisper, my hands aching to reach for her.

Her eyes dart up to mine, then they look past me almost as if she expects me to not be alone. I barely keep myself from huffing. She must not have much faith in me if she thinks I could ever spend another second of my life with any woman other than her.

I step aside, an invitation for her to come in but also proof that I'm here alone. She wavers on the threshold for a long moment before making her decision to enter.

She doesn't speak as she steps into the center of the room, turning to face me. I don't ruin the moment by speaking of regrets or begging her to stay like Robbie urged me to do days ago. Her mind is made up and so is mine. There's no turning back.

I watch her as she watches me, and I think we both make the decision at the same time. We know how this night ends.

Tears mark her pretty face, and I wish I could say that I'm able to keep mine dry, but that would be a lie. Our first kiss of the night is tainted with the salt of both of our tears as our lips meet, but it's not a hurried meeting of our mouths.

There's no rush. She's not making it to work tonight, and we both know it.

Clothes disappear a piece at a time, the fabric getting stripped away and fluttering to the floor at our feet.

My lips are soft on her skin, and I make damn sure to keep my teeth out of the equation this time because even nipping at her flesh would turn into biting. I want to punish her for the pain I've been feeling, for the torture we've both been suffering, but that wouldn't be fair. She's only doing what she feels is best for her child. I refuse to make her feel guilty for that.

Instead, I lick at her throat and suck on her nipples when she unclasps her bra. Working open her jeans, I drop to my knees and suck on her clit over the top of her panties. Her fingers tangle in my hair, the gasps and groans escaping her lips the sexiest sounds I've ever heard.

It's hard not praising her, begging her to come on my lips, but I don't want words to ruin the moment.

I tug off her shoes before I peel her panties down her legs, making sure to hold her up. I don't want her toppling over. She won't get on the bed until I put her there myself. Everything is spinning out of control, but this is one thing I can have power over, one place I can make decisions.

I lift one of her legs, placing the crook of her knee over my shoulder, opening her center up to me, and I spend a long minute just looking at her, memorizing the sight of her. Sweet, pink, and swollen with need. She glistens with arousal, the dim light in the hotel room doing nothing to diminish her appeal.

Her fingers flex against my scalp, a plea to stop torturing her, but it's the least I can do. I blow a stream of air on her naked flesh, but when she jolts in my arms, I can no longer resist. The first sweep of my tongue over her slit is all it takes to turn me ravenous.

I groan when the taste of her hits the back of my throat, and I know my grip on her ass is going to leave marks, but it doesn't make me loosen my hold on her. We may only have tonight, but I want her to remember me for the rest of her life. When she's in the shower, alone in bed, when her fingers roam down her stomach, I want this moment on her mind. When she sees a man noticing her, I want her to look at him knowing no one will do this as well as I can. I want her ruined, spoiled for all others. I want her knowing nothing else will compare.

She trembles, her knees buckling, but her leg over my shoulder won't allow her to topple. I've got her now, and I'd have her forever if she'd just let me.

The fingers of one hand slides between her ass cheeks, on a mission to find that soaked slit of hers, and it's an easy task. I'm going to have a bald spot, I realize when she tugs on my hair as I slip two fingers inside of her. The angle is awkward, but I'm good at improvising. I curl them the right way, and it sends her over the edge.

The rhythmic grip of her pussy on my fingers is a promise of what's coming later for my cock, but tonight, I need a little of everything from her.

As I stand, I drop her leg and add just the slightest amount of pressure to her shoulders. She obeys the wordless command just as I hoped she would, her hands going to the zipper of my jeans as she lowers herself to her knees. I'm shirtless, anticipating her arrival, and I'm not wearing my boots. I knew if she showed up tonight, I was going to end up inside of her, and I wasn't wasting time on pretenses.

Her lips are around the head of my cock the second the tip hits the air, and I groan at the warmth of her mouth. My jeans are tangled around my calves, but I'll worry about getting them completely off later. I do my best to use a gentle hand on the back of her head. The woman requires no fucking guidance when she's doing this. Even the periodic scrape of her teeth on the underside of me feels intentional.

I'll come too quickly if I'm not careful, and that isn't how I want things to end tonight. With one hand gripping the base of me, fingers tight and twisting, her other hand digs into my thigh. I tremble, legs shaking, muscles tight with pleasure and need. It's bliss, the feel of her suction and release.

I tilt my face up, the sight of her too much to watch. The swarm in my gut starts that low burn deep inside that can't be ignored, and I have to shift my hips back. I fall heavily from her mouth. Her lips are swollen, wet with a combination of her own saliva and my precum.

I kick my jeans the rest of the way off as I reach for her, my lips meeting hers the second she stands, and I want to get lost in her. I want to forget the rest of the world if only for an hour or so, but I refuse to compromise her future, to take away her choice and complicate her life any further.

I take a step back, loving the way she reaches for me in the distance I create as I reach for my jeans and produce a condom from the pocket. She watches, her teeth digging into her delicate lower lip as I roll the barrier down my length. She put the boundary between us when she chose going to Texas over staying and having a family with me. If she hadn't, I wouldn't worry with the damn thing.

I try not to be too rough with that reminder in my head when I lift her from the floor. By the time I press her back to the bed, I'm mostly under control once again.

I both want and need hard and fast. I want and need soft and slow. I'm at war with the two, a battle inside. I want to beg, but I also want to punish.

Her eyes beg me, and as well as I've gotten to know this woman, I don't know what she's asking for. Does she want the punishment, or is she needing forgiveness?

I give her soft and slow because I don't want our last memories together to leave a sour taste in her mouth. I press my lips to hers, lining my cock up at her entrance. That part of me has no doubts. It knows exactly what to do and pleasing her is its only mission. It's doesn't want to maim and hurt. It doesn't want to burn the world down and leave casualties lying around. It's only looking for pleasure. I obey him, drawing out her whimpers and gasps, smiling into her throat when her legs open further before she wraps her legs high on my hips.

My thrusts are slow and purposeful, the grind at the top for her gratification, the soft sound she makes because of it for mine. Sweat slicks our skin, sticking us to each other as we become a single entity in more ways than one.

I don't allow myself to picture us being more than that. Letting go tonight is already going to be too hard as it is. I live in the moment, the right now, and I seize what I can from here, breathing her in, memorizing every single second.

Her orgasm takes me by surprise, the slow roll of her hips the only warning I get before her body begins to tremble and that promise she made on my fingers becomes a reality as she pulses down the length of my cock. My hips slow as I fuck her through it, moaning in her ear because, fuck, she feels so damn good.

I follow shortly after. I couldn't hold back after that if I wanted to. Her body calls to mine like we were meant for—

No. I can't even think thoughts like that. They're not allowed.

The hope I had before she arrived, that idea I prayed for that she was going to tell me that she changed her mind, that she was going to choose me, died the second I opened the door and saw the look in her eyes.

She made her choice, and now I have to follow through with mine.

She clings to me a second longer when I try to pull away. I give it to her. I stay locked against her chest, kissing her tears away, not hiding the ones that fall from my own eyes.

Goodbyes fucking suck, and I know that this is going to be the last one. I'll never do it again.

As much as I wanted to ruin her for other men, she's done that very same fucking thing for me. No other woman would compare to her.

A chance meeting in a gas station parking lot, and Lucy Farrow changed my world forever.

Broken right to the center of me, I have to pull away.

She wastes no time climbing out of the bed, and I don't try to stop her.

We don't speak as she dresses, and I dispose of the condom.

Her tears are silent, much like the entire night has been other than me saying her name when she first arrived. She doesn't apologize for the pain or her choices, and I don't expect her to. Much like I won't apologize for the things I said back at the clubhouse. I meant them in the moment, and I still mean them now. Robbie doesn't deserve the blind following he's getting, and Harley deserves better, but the decisions she makes about her son are hers.

Fully dressed, she pauses at the door. I don't know if she's giving me the opportunity to try and stop her again or what, but I don't open my mouth.

She shocks me when she turns back around to face me with a gentle smile.

I smile back, my heart in pieces.

"It's going to be okay, sweetheart," I tell her, and as I say the words, I know it to be true with every part of me. "Tell Harley I said hello."

She nods, the tears falling more heavily now. She clears her throat, her head shaking like she wants to speak but she doesn't know if she'll be able to. "I can't stay, but I already don't want to leave."

I know she's talking about right now, but it feels like she means New Mexico, and I wish that made me feel just a little better.

It doesn't.

"I understand, sweetheart." It's the first and only time I'll lie to her.

She dips her head as a small sob escapes her lips, and then Lucy walks away from me.

Chapter 21

Lucy

Bad days happen.

For me, they happen often.

I don't really count them or consider them bad omens.

But when bad days happen on the day I'm starting a new life, it doesn't really lend me much faith that the move to Texas is the right choice.

Harley's first plane ride is also my first plane ride, and right now we're having to circle the airport in Houston because of some issue on the ground. I'm nervous, and he's irritable. We had to get up early and drive to Albuquerque to catch our flight, and we somehow still managed to nearly miss it because of airport security being slow.

Robbie is flying back to New Mexico in a couple weeks to sell my car, and he didn't give me a straight answer about how we're supposed to get around in the time being in Texas. It feels like my early twenties all over again, and we're flying by the seat of our pants. Only now, we have a kid we're responsible for.

I never thought I had a problem with other people's children, but it only took about thirty minutes into a two-hour flight with a crying toddler before I swore off ever having another child.

"How much longer?" Harley whines, his nose resting on the windowsill.

"I don't know, buddy. Hopefully not long."

As if someone is answering menial prayers today, the captain comes on the loudspeaker and tells us that we just got clearance to land. A cheer goes up through the plane, and it makes me feel a little better that I wasn't the only one annoyed with the delay. Honestly, I was more worried about running out of gas and falling from the sky.

Landing is just as uneventful as taking off, and I follow everyone else's lead on how we're supposed to file off the airplane. Harley and I follow the people through the airport, doing our best to watch for the signs directing us to where our luggage can be picked up at.

"Potty?" I ask Harley when he does that little dance.

He nods, heading for the restroom with the image of the guy.

"Fat chance," I say, holding his head and turning him toward the women's restroom.

He huffs, but there's not a chance I'm letting my six-year-old go into a men's restroom alone. I don't care how many looks I get from women who have an opinion on the matter. The child needs to pee. He's not going to be crawling on the nasty floor looking under the damn doors, and if women are in any form of undress in a public bathroom and don't mind being seen by other women, they sure as hell shouldn't worry about a child neither.

I feel mad and indignant as we enter the restroom, and that's just another hint that I've already had a full day and it's barely noon. No one gives us a second look other than a kind-looking grandmotherly person who grins at Harley as he rushes into a stall, a chuckle escaping her lips when he makes a noise of pure relief as he makes it in time.

"He's a little dramatic," I tell her.

"I must be too, because I did the exact same thing," she says as she dries her hands on a paper towel. "Have a good day, dear."

While I wait for Harley to finish and wash his hands, I turn my cell phone off of airplane mode, and it chimes immediately with texts messages.

Robbie: Don't freak out.

Robbie: My new boss just told me the duplex was accidentally given to someone else.

Robbie: But they found something else.

Robbie: This is the new address. 5609 Crescent Square.

Robbie: Don't get a cab. There will be a car waiting for you.

Robbie: Please message me back and tell me you aren't freaking out.

Robbie: You were supposed to land forty minutes ago.

Robbie: Lucy?

Robbie: Are you two, okay?

Robbie: LUCY?

Robbie: LUCY!

"Momma?"

I look down at Harley.

"What's wrong?"

I shake my head. "Nothing."

Chances are the house we're being sent to isn't furnished. Chances are all the things I had shipped here last week have either been stolen or sold. Chances are Robbie's choices have screwed me over again.

"Are you ready?"

Everything in me is telling me to use every penny I have to head to the ticket counter and buy us plane tickets back to New Mexico, but I know for a fact the landlord already has tenants lined up to move into the house we vacated. I doubt Micah will ever look at me again, and I'm not even sure the money I have is enough to get the both of us home.

I huff a humorless laugh as I grab the handle to my rolling carry-on and shove my phone in my back pocket. I'll think about messaging Robbie back when I calm down. I slip my other hand into Harley's.

"Ready?"

He shrugs. "Do I have a choice?"

"Not really?" I scrunch my nose at him, a little hint that I'm not as excited as I've tried to pretend recently. If anything, we'll still be on the same team. If we get to that new address and there's an issue, I'll just turn around and leave. I won't put Harley in a bad situation. If I can walk away from a good man because I feel like it's in his best interest, I can walk away from his father if it's in his best interest as well.

Our checked luggage is already circling the carousel when we approach, and a nice gentleman helps me pull it off when he notices me struggling. I thank him and walk outside, smiling at a man in a suit when Harley points, noticing him holding a sign with our last name on it.

"Harley and Lucy?" the man asks as we approach.

"That's us!" Harley says, sounding excited for the first time in weeks.

Weirdness settles in my bones. I wasn't looking forward to the expense of taking a cab for the hour-long ride from the airport to Galveston, but Robbie doesn't have a car. Being driven in a hired car must be even more expensive, and it makes me wonder if my ex is actually working for an offshore oil rig or he's gotten tangled up in something a little more sinister.

Did he get involved in something terrible while he was in prison? I'd like to believe he wouldn't let Harley get involved in something like that, but at the end of the day, do I really know the man? We were high when he was on the outside, and I only got to see what he wanted me to see while he was locked up.

The man places our bags in the trunk of the car and holds the back door open for us. Whoever hired the company was thoughtful enough to have a booster seat installed in the back, and Harley wastes no time settling in and pulling the seatbelt so I can lock it in place.

"Ready?" the driver asks when he takes a seat behind the wheel.

"Yes," Harley answers.

"Ma'am, your seatbelt?"

I rush to put it on, pulling my phone from my back pocket before snapping it into place.

"You have the new address?" I ask, pulling up the text thread with my ex.

"5609 Crescent Square," he confirms.

I nod.

"Yes, ma'am."

He pulls away. My mind is racing as we drive toward the ocean. Harley seems content to watch the traffic, and I'm grateful he didn't ask questions when I confirmed the address.

Me: You have a lot of explaining to do.

Robbie doesn't respond, and my mood is more than sour as Houston starts to fade behind us and things turn more industrial.

The air in the vehicle is thick, and I'm sure that's all my fault, but there's no conversation, and the radio isn't even on. I'm doing my best to determine if the man driving seems like a hired car or if he's the type of man to work full-time for a drug cartel. I don't notice any neck tattoos. His hands are free of ink, but then I feel like a jerk. Micah is covered in tattoos, and he's not a criminal. I don't think Robbie has any ink, at least he didn't before he went to prison, and he's got numerous offenses on his record, so judging books by those covers doesn't always pan out.

Robbie: I'm doing paperwork for human resources, but the key will be under the mat.

We cross a long bridge before taking an exit. Harley gasps at the ocean, but I know from doing research on my phone that it's not the real ocean. Galveston, on most days, isn't what he's probably imagining. It's not pristine beaches with sparkling blue water. It's the gulf and always a little dirty.

Several turns later, the car begins to slow before stopping completely.

"Ma'am?"

I look to the driver to see him nod out the passenger side.

The house he directs my attention to is adorable, painted a seafoam green with a little white fence around it. The entire house is trimmed in white. The porch is huge, and without even craning my neck, I can tell that the backyard is the beach, the ocean not very far from that.

"This isn't the right house," I mutter as Harley unsnaps his seatbelt and climbs into my lap. His breath fogs up the window.

"This is 5609 Crescent Square."

"I love this house, Momma."

I do too, I think, but I'd never say it out loud because this is a mistake.

"I'll get your luggage," the driver says as he opens his door.

"Can you just wait?" I ask, as I type out a text.

Me: This is a mistake. This can't be where I'm supposed to live. I can't afford this house, Robbie.

I climb out of the car because Harley is a ball of energy, but I manage to catch him by the arm before he races up the front porch.

"Please wait for me," I tell him.

The driver waits by the back of the car for further instruction.

"Momma," Harley groans in complaint. "You didn't tell me there was a swing set."

I can see it around the side of the house as well, but I won't let him go to go check it out.

Robbie hasn't texted me back. Of course he hasn't. Why would he actually be present while any of this was going on?

I reread the text thread, looking up and seeing the welcome mat near the front door.

Before checking the numbers on the house, I turn back to the driver.

"You're sure this is the right house?"

He nods.

"And there isn't a 5609 Crescent Drive or 5609 Crescent Road in a less expensive neighborhood?"

"I can check."

I wait on the front walk with a squirming little boy beside me as the driver pulls out his cell phone. The wait seems to take forever.

"There's not another Crescent anything in Galveston Texas, ma'am. This is the only one."

"Thank you." I look down at Harley. "Stay right beside me, understand?"

He nods. I walk slowly up the front porch steps, bending to look under the mat, and right where Robbie texted it would be is the key. It's like I'm living in the damn twilight zone. I pick it up, but I don't insert it into the lock.

I knock on the front door.

"You have a key. Why are you knocking?" Harley asks like I'm crazy.

I'm feeling a little crazy right now.

The front door is just as gorgeous as the rest of the property, more glass than wood, a beautiful, beveled floral design. I don't think I would've noticed the movement inside the house if I weren't looking at it so intently. I knock again, but no one comes to the door. Like a weirdo, I press my nose to the glass, hoping it will help me see better. It doesn't.

All I can make out is a huge shape standing right in the middle of the entryway.

"Use the key, Momma."

"Someone is in there," I say.

"Ask them if I can play on the swing set."

"Get back," I hiss when the shape moves.

Sensing my fear, Harley moves in front of me before I can shift to protect him.

I don't know when he deemed himself my protector, but the forty-pound little guy puffs out his chest as the door swings open.

"Micah!" Harley screams.

I'm speechless, tears burning my eyes at the sight of him.

Harley doesn't waste a second jumping into his arms, just like Micah doesn't waste a second crouching to catch him. I lose the sight of his magnificent blue eyes as they flutter closed when he hugs my son, his arms wrapped all the way around his tiny frame.

"Hey, sweetheart," he whispers, shifting Harley to one hip as he reaches for me with his free hand. "Welcome home."

Harley rests his head on Micah's shoulder as if it's the most natural thing in the world, and I get the sudden urge to pinch myself, terrified that I've fallen asleep on the plane, and I'm dreaming.

"What are you doing here?"

"I love you, woman. Do you really think I was going to let you move to Texas without me?"

I blink up at him. "Love?"

"Like a lot," he says with a wide grin.

"Micah, there's a swing set out back."

Micah looks from me to my son. "And an ocean. Wanna check it out?" Harley nods, wiggling to be set free.

"Through there." He points toward a door at the back of the house. "But just the swing set for right now."

"What is—"

He presses his fingers to my mouth, silencing me.

"We have a million things to talk about, and we'll get to them, but first—"

He covers my mouth with his, tongue sweeping inside. I groan, gripping his shirt as his hands grip my ass.

A cough pulls us apart.

"Sir?"

Micah chuckles against my mouth, but he presses one more kiss to my lips before pulling completely away.

The driver is standing there beside all our luggage. Micah pulls his wallet out and hands the man some cash. "Thanks, Brandon."

"Anytime, Mr. Cobreski."

The guy walks to the car and drives off.

"I know you didn't want me to stay the night at your house, but I'm inviting you two to stay the night at mine."

"I'm guessing Robbie wasn't lying about the duplex being rented?"

"Your half of the duplex was rented. Robbie still has the other half. He's about three miles away."

"And you two set this up together?"

"He was told what was going to happen." He gives me a small smile. "He didn't put up much of a fight. I'm not going to stir shit up with your ex, baby, but I can tell you that we're going to have to keep a close eye on him. I hope for Harley's sake that the man is on the right path, but I'm not so sure he is."

I nod my head because I've had my own doubts.

I walk toward him, my arms going around his waist. "I can't even begin to tell you how happy I am that you're here, but what about your life back in New Mexico?"

"I couldn't live without the two of you, Lucy. Once I realized that, the decision was easy."

"And Cerberus?"

"Kincaid would've kicked my ass if I let you walk away."

"Really?" I look up at him as he presses a kiss to my forehead.

"He literally used those very words. I have friends all over the world. I've got something lined up at a bike shop here in town."

"So my assumption about bikers in the beginning wasn't too far off, huh?"

His rumbled laughter against my chest makes me smile.

"We better get out back before that boy chooses today as the day he's going to start misbehaving."

I wrap my arm around his waist and let him guide me to the backyard. Harley is nothing but smiles and happiness as he pumps his legs, the swing he's sitting on going back and forth.

"Do you like it?" Micah asks.

"Love it," Harley says. "Is all of my stuff here?"

"It's at your dad's place," Micah answers.

I'm glad I don't have to repurchase everything.

The swing slows as Harley's face starts to fall.

"What's wrong? Tired already?"

"Hey, kiddo?" Micah prompts when he doesn't answer me. "Your momma asked a question."

He hasn't been around to see the shift in his attitude the last couple of weeks, and I hate that he's witnessing it now. It makes me feel even more like a failure. I've always been so proud of how well behaved he's been.

"We're not going to live here?" Harley kicks at the sand under his feet.

Micah puts me on the spot, turning to look at me, his head cocked a little to the side.

"I live here," Micah says, his words directed at Harley, but his eyes turned to me.

I narrow mine at him, noticing the smile he's trying to hide.

"There are only two bedrooms," the man adds.

"Okay," Harley says slowly.

I wait for the kid to offer to sleep on the couch, but then he surprises me completely.

"I'll take the smaller one, and you two can have the bigger one. Problem solved."

"Problem solved," Micah says, walking over to Harley and giving him a high-five.

When leaving the airport, I was sure that Harley and I were on a team. Looking at the two of them, I know a team has been formed, I just didn't know I was going to be on the outside of it.

"Is that right?" I ask, crossing my arms over my chest.

They look at each other, comic smiles on their faces before looking back at me and nodding.

"Well, maybe the boys need to share a room, and the girl gets her own room."

Harley's eyes go wide. Micah's narrow.

"We could get bunk beds," Harley whispers, like it's the best idea in the world.

"We need to discuss this," Micah tells my son. "You go back to swinging."

I feel like prey when he prowls toward me, but I hold my ground.

"How much is it going to break his heart when I tell him I'm sleeping in a bed with you?"

I shrug. "Not much. Just mention that you wouldn't be comfortable in a bunk bed because you're so big. He's a compassionate kid. He wouldn't want you to be in pain."

"I'm still going to spank your ass later for putting the idea in his head."

"Can't wait," I tell him with a wink.

"Micah!" Harley says, his swing soaring through the air. "Can I be a biker for Cerberus when I grow up?"

"Gotta be a Marine first, kiddo."

"Is that all?" he asks.

"That's it."

"Sounds like a plan," my son says.

Epilogue

Harley

25 years later

Growing up, my mom protected me from a lot of things.

I knew we didn't have a lot of money, but the important things were always readily available. I had hugs and food. She always smiled. I only caught her crying a couple of times.

I thought she was happy.

I didn't realize how truly unhappy she was in life until she met Micah "Snake" Cobreski.

Until then, a lot of her smiles were fake. At six years old and before, I didn't know a smile couldn't reach your eyes. I didn't know that laughter could be fake, and that she was never allergic to lemons. That her red, puffy eyes when she picked me up from Mrs. Greene's house with those excuses were the nights that were just too bad and she spent a lot of them crying.

She was willing to give up that man for me, and I think if things turned out that way in the end, I might have ended up hating her a little. Micah didn't let that happen. That man came into our lives like a battering ram, and I'm the man I am today because of it.

I wouldn't have served twelve years in the Marine Corps if it weren't for him.

I wouldn't trust my heart with Lana, my wife of six years.

I never would've found the courage to be a good father to Aria, my precious two-month-old daughter if it wasn't for the example he set for me.

I got nothing from my biological father.

Of course I remember the visits with him in prison, the man he tried to be, the advice he tripped over, the example he tried to set after uprooting us from New Mexico in the middle of first grade.

Thank God, Micah met us in Galveston because by that very summer, my father was on drugs and had been fired from the job that brought us to Texas in the first place. Micha was our rock, our touchstone, the example I learned to live by. I appreciate him in more ways than I'll ever be able to find the words to say.

It wasn't all butterflies and roses. I was stubborn growing up and used the words *you're not my father* more than once, but he stuck with me. He never told me he wished he'd made a different decision when my mother left him because she thought I needed more time with Robert Farrow. The man adopted me when Robert thought giving up his full rights when I was nine would be easier than being responsible for child support.

I owe Micah everything.

Guilt settles inside of me as the minister finishes his generic speech.

I don't bother to watch as the casket is lowered into the ground.

"Are you okay?" Lana asks as we walk back toward my truck.

"I'm fine," I answer honestly.

It's not the complete truth, but I know what she's referring to, and it isn't my guilt about being here. She wants to know where my head is at emotionally, and I'm fine with what I just sat through, if not a little annoyed to have had to arrange my day around the graveside service.

"Are you sure? Your dad just died."

I take a sleeping Aria from her arms and place her gently into the rear-facing infant seat in the back of the truck.

"My dad is with my mom somewhere in the Caribbean for the second time this winter. I barely knew that man."

I'm actually shocked it took Robert Farrow until the age of fifty-four to finally overdose. The greater shock is that he wasn't in prison when it happened. I haven't kept tabs on him at all, so to get the call from a hospital in San Antonio—only three hours away from where we live in Houston—five days ago was a surprise.

I called my dad—Micah. He's been that to me since the day he adopted me, and I asked for advice. I was planning to just let the state deal with him, but he said the right thing to do would be to take care of it, that if I regretted spending a little money, I could always make more money. If I turned my back on it, the regret later on couldn't be remedied. The man never steered me wrong in the past.

So I made the preparations—a graveside service, a basic headstone, a minister whose name I don't know that didn't know him. It's more than he ever did for me.

Lana's hand comes down on my arm, and like it always has, it has the power to calm everything inside of me.

"Tell me you're okay."

"Baby." I pull her to my chest and press my lips to her forehead. "I've got you and my little girl. Life is perfect."

"Almost perfect," she counters. "In a week, the last part of your dream comes true."

I grin against the top of her head because she's got a point.

I remember the declaration I made the first day Mom and I showed up in Galveston. I told Micah I wanted to be a biker with the Cerberus MC. At the time, I had no idea what that meant. At six, I thought it was riding motorcycles and having fun. As a man with a family he values over anything in the world, I know what they do, what their mission is, and I want it even more.

Next week, I sign my contract with that very club, and even though we aren't blood related, I'm still joining the Cerberus MC.

I get to carry on the legacy.

I'm Harley Cobreski.

I'm Cerberus.

THE END

OTHER BOOKS FROM MARIE JAMES

Newest Series
Blackbridge Security
Hostile Territory
Shot in the Dark
Contingency Plan
Truth Be Told
Calculated Risk
Heroic Measures
Sleight of Hand
Controlled Burn
Cease Fire

Standalones
Crowd Pleaser
Macon
We Said Forever
More Than a Memory

Cole Brothers SERIES
Love Me Like That
Teach Me Like That

Cerberus MC
Kincaid: Cerberus MC Book 1
Kid: Cerberus MC Book 2
Shadow: Cerberus MC Book 3
Dominic: Cerberus MC Book 4
Snatch: Cerberus MC Book 5
Lawson: Cerberus MC Book 6
Hound: Cerberus MC Book 7
Griffin: Cerberus MC Book 8
Samson: Cerberus MC Book 9
Tug: Cerberus MC Book 10
Scooter: Cerberus MC Book 11
Cannon: Cerberus MC Book 12
Rocker: Cerberus MC Book 13
Colton: Cerberus MC Book 14
Drew: Cerberus MC Book 15
Jinx: Cerberus MC Book 16
Thumper: Cerberus MC Book 17
Apollo: Cerberus MC Book 18
Legend: Cerberus MC Book 19
Grinch: Cerberus MC Book 20
Harley: Cerberus MC Book 21
A Very Cerberus Christmas
Cerberus MC Box Set 1
Cerberus MC Box Set 2
Cerberus MC Box Set 3

Ravens Ruin MC
Desperate Beginnings: Prequel
Grab it for free HERE!

Book 1: Sins of the Father
Book 2: Luck of the Devil
Book 3: Dancing with the Devil

MM Romance
Grinder
Taunting Tony

Westover Prep Series
(bully/enemies to lovers romance)
One-Eighty
Catch Twenty-Two

Made in the USA
Columbia, SC
07 June 2024

36781021R00080